D0952638

CRUEL
FATE

CRUEL FATE

A CAINSVILLE NOVELLA

KELLEY ARMSTRONG

Illustrations by Xavière Daumarie

SUBTERRANEAN PRESS 2019

First Edition

ISBN
978-1-59606-906-0

Subterranean Press
PO Box 190106
Burton, MI 48519

subterraneanpress.com

Manufactured in the United States of America

THE WATCHER

A LONE figure stood outside the maximum-security prison, a cheap duffel bag at his feet, his hands pushed deep into his pockets. With each passing car, he'd straighten, only to deflate again when it continued on.

Signs along the road warned against picking up hitchhikers. An escaped convict, though, would stand a little farther from the prison gates. This man had been released. His sentence complete, freedom granted, meager belongings in that crumpled bag, now all he needed was someone to pick him up and take him home. And no one was coming.

Arianell moved closer, weed trimmer screeching as she… Well, she had no idea what she was doing with it. From the name of the device, one would presume she was supposed to be trimming weeds. There weren't any here, and this was where she needed to be, so she waved the device around and cut down grass instead.

The released prisoner glanced her way only briefly. Her stolen maintenance uniform swam around her thin frame, pooling over the outsized work boots. She'd set her fae glamour to gray-haired and wrinkled, and while the man by the roadside may have spent twenty-plus woman-free years in prison, she still wasn't worthy of a second glance. He'd looked. He'd dismissed. He'd already forgotten. Conveniently.

She made her way closer, approaching from the rear as he faced the road. She'd gotten only a glimpse of his face, but she knew her target. Blond hair, worn a little long for his age. A slight build and oversized jacket that hid the physique of a man who'd spent two decades visiting the prison gym.

She approached with care. This human had fae blood, and if she set off his internal alarms, he could handle her in this old lady form. While the justice system had now declared him innocent of eight deaths, they'd missed one. The murder he'd actually committed.

Todd Larsen knew how to take care of himself. And so she had to proceed with extreme caution.

When tires rumbled, Todd's head jerked up. Then he realized the sound came from inside the prison lot, and his shoulders slumped.

Arianell's eyes narrowed as she watched.

Such a pity, Todd. Your daughter might have fought to get you free, but when those gates finally opened, she's nowhere to be seen. I'm sure she'll show up...eventually. After her manicure, perhaps. You're alone out here, Todd, and that means you're vulnerable. Alone and—

A red Maserati peeled from the prison, windows down, a man's laugh ringing out. It'd barely cleared the gates before it veered to the curb.

The driver's door opened, and two knee-high boots appeared, followed by a young woman in sunglasses, her ash blond hair swinging. She leaned back in and dangled the car keys.

"Come on," she said. "You drive."

The passenger door opened. A man climbed out. He was older than the girl, with dark blond hair not unlike the man standing at the gates. He was about the same size, too, perhaps slightly wider in the shoulders, slightly taller.

He laughed as he shook his head. "My license expired a very long time ago, Liv."

"So?" She waved the keys. "You know you wanna."

"Sure, but do you know what I *don't* want? To get arrested fifty feet outside the prison gates."

The man standing by the gate grumbled and shoved his hands deeper into his pockets as he turned away from the scene. He glanced at Arianell, and she got her first good look at his face...at least a decade younger than she expected.

"What are you staring at?" he snapped.

"Not much," she murmured and then said, under her breath, "Not Todd Larsen."

Todd Larsen was the guy standing by the Maserati, the man joking and laughing with his daughter. Olivia, Liv, Eden, Matilda... whatever name the young woman went by these days.

So she had come to pick Todd up. That didn't mean she'd keep a careful watch over him. And when she didn't, Arianell would be there.

She watched the two climb back into the car, Olivia in the driver's seat. Then she stalked away to return the stolen clothes before the groundskeeper regained consciousness.

ONE

OLIVIA

"STEAK," I said to Todd as I sped through the streets of Chicago. "That's what you asked for, and that's what you're getting."

"Uh, I joked that steak would be my death row meal if Illinois brought back the death penalty."

"Well, that's off the table forever now. No last meal. Just a first one, for which you are having steak at the best restaurant in town."

"Not Ponderosa, then?"

I laughed. "I'm not sure those are still around."

"You used to love Ponderosa. You weren't old enough for steak, but you went nuts for the potato and ice-cream bar. I'm not sure which you liked more."

I smiled over at him. My father. Finally here, finally free. He'd gone to prison, along with my mother, when I was two and a half. They'd been convicted of killing eight people. Murderers that my mother had killed in a fae deal to fix the severe spina bifida that had crippled me. We still hoped to get my mother free, but for now, I had my father.

"Eyes on the road, Liv," he said. "I may not have driven in twenty-three years, but I know that part is important."

"Yes, sir."

"As for lunch, we don't have to—"

"Yep, we totally do. We are celebrating."

"Am I dressed okay? How fancy is this place?"

"You are. That's why I brought clothes for you. It's lunch. Business casual is fine. There's a sports jacket in the back if you want it."

When he didn't reply, I gripped the wheel tighter. My stomach buzzed and flipped, half with giddy excitement and half with abject terror. My father was free, finally free, and it fell on me to make sure everything went perfectly.

"Smoothly," Gabriel had corrected last night when I confessed my fears. *"The goal is smoothly, not perfectly. Even then there will be bumps—"*

I silenced Gabriel's warnings and turned to my father, ready to say we could skip lunch if he wanted. He was gazing out the window, and when he turned, he smiled.

"Looks a little different out there," he said.

I swallowed. "I know it might be…unsettling. It's been so long."

My entire life. He had spent almost my entire lifetime in a prison cell. Everything he remembered came before my time. My world was not his.

He smiled again, that easy, reassuring smile. "I've had access to television, Liv. TV, movies, books, even that thing they call the Internet." His eyes glittered, teasing now. "I haven't stepped out of a time machine. Or even a bomb shelter." He leaned back in his seat. "I do remember seeing these old Maseratis in Chicago, though. They were antiques even then. The kind of car my friends and I drooled over."

"And you can drive this one as soon as you have your license," I said. "I've researched the procedure." I'd researched *every* procedure, every way to get Todd's life back on track. "You'll need to be retested, but we'll work on that. Then you'll have your license and a very nice car to go with it. My dad...I mean, my—"

"Your dad," Todd said firmly. "Arthur Jones raised you and did an awesome job, and I'm happy to share the title with him."

I nodded. "What I was saying was that he left me all his cars. They're just sitting in our old garage, gathering dust. Lots of antiques. Lots of sports cars. You can take your pick."

When Todd said nothing, I glanced over. "They're mine," I said firmly. "He would want them driven."

"What about the Jetta?" he asked. "That's the one you were driving before the Maserati, isn't it?"

"The housekeeper's old car, yes. It's running—again—after Gabriel disabled it to force me to take this one."

Todd chuckled. "Did he finally admit to it?"

"Never. But you don't need to take that one. There's—"

"I'll learn on that. I had a VW. An old bug. I'd like the Jetta."

His voice—quiet but firm—told me not to argue, and I didn't. I pulled up in front of the steak house and climbed out.

"Valet parking?" Todd said with a low whistle. "I did that exactly once, when I proposed to your mom. I had no idea how it worked, so I stood around waiting for the guy to bring my key back. Then I realized I'd left the engagement ring box in the car. It's a miracle she said yes."

A miracle? That's not what I'd call marrying a woman whose crimes sent you to prison for half your life. All she had to do was confess, and he'd have been free. Todd never wanted that, though. If Pamela confessed, she'd lose her chance at freedom, and she'd been in there for doing something he couldn't. He'd set my cure in motion, taking the life of Gregory Kirkman—a serial killer—and that had horrified him enough that he hadn't been able to go through with the rest. So Pamela had. I got my cure. He got a life sentence.

Todd didn't see it that way. He'd loved Pamela. Still cared about her. She was my mother, and she'd done what she thought was right, and if there'd been any anger, he'd long since gotten over it. He wanted her free, even if he never talked about reuniting.

Before the valet took the car, Todd grabbed the sports coat from the back. He put it on, tugging and fussing like a man who had only worn them to weddings and funerals even before his incarceration. Todd grew up in a working-class family, finished high school, became a carpenter, married my mother at twenty, with me appearing a year later. He'd gotten exactly what he wanted from life and had considered himself unbelievably lucky to have it all so young.

"Tie?" he asked as he fastened his top button.

I reached over and undid the button. "Nope. Leave it like that, and come on. We have reservations, and I am starving."

He held the door for me. As I walked in, I looked around and made a face. This wasn't quite the atmosphere I'd hoped for. Gabriel and I usually came for dinner, and even if we stopped by earlier, it'd be a late lunch, after the crowds had left, the restaurant elegant and subdued. Today it was lunch hour midweek, and the place sounded like a stock exchange floor, with guys in suits doing business at top volume, waving their steak knives for emphasis.

I followed the maître d' through that gauntlet of knives. Most saw me coming and pulled in their weapons. A few looked me over, their gazes starting at my boots and not rising above my neckline.

The maître d' stopped mid-dining room, and pulled out a chair for me.

"I requested the fireplace room," I said. "The corner table."

"I am afraid—" he began.

"I reserved it a month ago."

My voice never rose. There was no edge to it, no snap. My adoptive parents had been bringing me to fancy restaurants since I was four. They had money, status and position, and I'd been raised a socialite. I knew how to deal with situations like this, calmly but firmly. Yet Todd shifted his weight, uncomfortable, as he murmured, "This is fine, Liv."

"Is there anyplace more private?" I asked.

The maître d' looked around the packed restaurant.

I nodded curtly and accepted the proffered chair. As we sat, the maître d' offered a complimentary glass of house wine. I shook my head but thanked him, my adoptive mother's training taking over. It was also her hand in my upbringing that made me refuse, and I don't appreciate that part, the ingrained snobbery that says you don't drink house wine and certainly not because it's free.

Todd pulled out his chair and sat awkwardly, his body tense, gaze flitting about. I'd wanted to treat him to a special first meal, and now I realized I'd brought him somewhere he wouldn't have been comfortable even before he went to prison. Yet another reminder of the gulf between us. A reminder to him that this was the world his daughter grew up in and inhabited effortlessly. And the worst of it? I'd picked the steak house because I didn't want anything *too* fancy.

Gabriel tried to warn me. He'd broached the subject with none of his usual blunt honesty. He knew how important this meal was, and so he'd tap-danced around the subject, as best Gabriel could tap-dance.

"Perhaps dinner out isn't what your father will want right away, Olivia. I've found an excellent steak house that will cater lunch to the condo. We can certainly go out later in the week if he—"

No, no, and nope. I wasn't hiding my father away from the world the moment he stepped back into it. He'd been acquitted, and we were celebrating.

"Please tell me inflation has been worse than I imagined," Todd said as he perused the menu. "Some of these steaks cost more than my old mortgage payments."

He smiled when he said it, but my gut twisted.

"They sound delicious, though," he hurried to say.

"This isn't how I usually eat," I said, "but when it comes to steak, I do indulge…and try not to think about how much I paid. First course, though, is drinks. Wine, cocktails, beer…"

"I don't think this is much of a beer joint."

I nodded to the table beside us where four young men sat with beer glasses. "Microbrews."

Todd's brows knitted.

"Small breweries, overpriced beer, very trendy." I paused. "Some of it is quite good. Tell me your usual brew, and I'll find a match."

"Miller Draft?"

I took out my phone and searched. "Miller Genuine Draft? It's a pale lager, right?"

He chuckled. "Not your kind of beer?"

I didn't tell him that, as popular as his brew had been in the eighties, it'd largely been discontinued. I scanned the drink menu and picked one that seemed appropriate. The server appeared, and I ordered that for Todd and a red wine for myself. I also got appetizers. By the time they arrived, we'd relaxed into conversation, Todd asking me what sorts of cases I was working on. I'm an investigator for Gabriel, who—as one of Chicago's most notorious defense attorneys—always has interesting cases. I was regaling Todd with a recent escapade, when a man approached. With my attention on

Todd, I only saw a suit take up position beside the table. I presumed it was a server, and so I finished my sentence before looking up to see a florid-faced man in his forties, his gaze fixed on my father.

"Todd Larsen," the man said, and there was a moment where Todd's brows furrowed, just a fraction, as if wondering whether he knew this man. Then he realized the man knew *him*...and why.

"Yes," Todd said carefully.

The man planted his hands on the table. "I didn't know this establishment served serial killers."

I resisted the urge to rise and said evenly, "Todd has been acquitted of all charges. He spent twenty-three years in prison for crimes he didn't commit."

The man's gaze traveled over me. "Huh. You're not wasting any time making up for those years, are you, Todd? Barely out of jail, and you're already buying yourself a steak dinner and a whore."

Todd's chair squealed back. Then he checked himself and pushed up slowly. "This is my daughter, though I'm sure you knew that. We're trying to enjoy—"

The man spat in Todd's beer. "Enjoy *that*, you murdering son of a bitch."

Todd picked up the glass. The man flinched. Then his face reddened as he realized he'd recoiled. Todd held the glass out to a passing server and said, "I'll need a fresh beer. There's something in this glass."

The woman had been hurrying past, not realizing what was happening. She stopped, her perfunctory server smile growing more genuine as she saw Todd.

"Absolutely, sir," she said. "I'm very sorry about that." She took the glass. "What were you drinking?"

"The blood of his victims," the red-faced man said. "That's what you did, wasn't it, Todd?" He turned to the server. "This guy you're making eyes at is a serial killer. He butchered girls like you. Raped their corpses. Drank their blood. Cut off their skin and ate it."

The restaurant fell silent, the server's face turning as white as her shirt. Before I could interject, a rumbling voice cut through the silence. "Could you repeat that? I'd like to be sure I have your exact words for when Mr. Larsen sues you for defamation."

I saw the top of Gabriel's head first, his wavy black hair moving above the knot of gathering onlookers. They parted for him. People always did. Gabriel was six foot four and built like a linebacker.

He walked over, expressionless, his unnaturally pale blue eyes chill but not cold. His gaze flicked to the red-faced man, who backed up.

"Don't go," Gabriel said. "You had something to say. Please repeat it."

The man didn't answer.

Gabriel continued. "My client was indeed wrongfully convicted of multiple murders. The death of four men and four women, murders that did *not* involve sexual assault or the drinking of blood or..." He fluttered his hand. "Whatever other lurid fantasies you concocted. I suggest you see a therapist about those."

A titter ran through the crowd. Gabriel walked over and kissed the side of my head. The public display of affection caught me off guard. Performance art, like the threat to sue. He discreetly squeezed my arm, and *that* was genuine, reassurance and support.

"I'm sorry I'm late," he said. "I was delayed in court." He looked at our table for two and chuckled again, more theater from a man who rarely even smiled in public. "And I see you'd given up on me. It seems unlikely we'll get another table. I'll dine elsewhere." A pause. "Unless you'd both care to join me?"

Gabriel was *not* late. He hadn't been coming to lunch with us. I'd asked whether he wanted to, but he'd demurred, saying this meal should be for Todd and me. I realized now that only meant he wasn't going to sit with us, not that he wouldn't be close by, making sure everything went as I hoped, leaping in when it didn't…as he'd expected.

Now he was offering an escape hatch. He knew that I, personally, wouldn't have let this guy spoil my lunch. Two years ago, Todd and Pamela had come back into my life, after I'd long forgotten them, forgotten I'd even been adopted. They'd returned in spectacular fashion, with a reporter outing me as the socialite daughter of serial killers. Then I went to work for the infamous Gabriel Walsh while dating a biker, and, *Oh, wait, now she's with the lawyer.* I'd done my time as a media bright-and-shiny. That meant this was not the first time—or the dozenth—that some asshole interrupted a meal to tell me what he really thought. I could be having the worst meal ever, the food barely edible, and I'd glue my ass to that chair and refuse to satisfy a tormentor by walking out.

But this was about Todd. Todd wasn't me, and he wasn't Gabriel, and he wasn't Pamela. He did not feel the need to grit his teeth and enjoy this meal in spite of himself.

"Sorry," I said as I rose. "They didn't have the table I reserved, and I thought you weren't able to join us. But since you are…"

I took his arm, and his lips twitched at that, as surprised as I'd been at his kiss of welcome. He nodded to Todd, telling him we'd follow him out. As we approached the front door, Gabriel cleared his throat.

"I'm parked around back," he said, and I glanced at the door, knowing what he really meant. Sure enough, two guys hovered at the entrance, cell phones in hand.

"Damn, that was fast," I murmured. "Okay, out the back, but I need to pay—"

"Done." He motioned toward the rear hall. "I left my credit card number in case you decided to cut the meal short."

As we walked into the rear hall, a young guy appeared from the kitchen, bag in hand. Gabriel took it with only a nod of acknowledgment, leaving me to say thanks.

"Lunch to go?" I said.

He nodded. "Again, in case..." He cleared his throat. "In case it was required."

We stepped out a door clearly marked No Exit, which led to a tiny parking lot where Gabriel had double-parked his Jag.

"My car's in the valet lot," I said.

"I know. However, your vehicle is not exactly unobtrusive. Take mine."

I nodded. The Jag opened as I tugged the handle.

He tucked the takeout into the back. "I need to run an errand, but I'll be home as soon as I can. I'm taking the afternoon off."

I squeezed his arm. "Thank you."

"You're very welcome."

⌇

AS we drove through the city, Todd said, "When I was your age, I'd have died for a ride in that sports car of yours. Maybe I'm just showing my age, but this?" He put the seat back, eyes closing as he sank into the leather of Gabriel's Jag. "*This* is my new idea of a dream car." He peeked over at the speedometer. "I see it doesn't have any problem with power, either."

I smiled. "This can outrun my Maserati with a much smoother ride and better handling. The advantage of modern automotive technology."

"It looks new, too."

"About eighteen months old. It's a replacement for one I wrecked." His brows lifted.

"We went down an embankment," I said. "*Rolled* down."

His gaze shot to the speedometer again.

"No," I said, "I wasn't driving too fast or taking a corner too sharp. Someone tried to kill us. It happens."

"I...see."

"It hasn't happened in a while, but make sure you wear your seatbelt just in case. And this model is awesome for rollovers. Lots of air bags. It's not a problem. Kind of fun. Inconvenient, though, replacing the car. Well, inconvenient for Gabriel."

He chuckled and shook his head.

My hands tightened on the wheel as I said, as lightly as possible, "So lunch was a bust."

"I'm sorry."

"No, *I'm* sorry. I didn't expect that, and I should have."

"You wanted to give me a special first meal. Now I have it." He hooked his thumb at the takeout bag. "And I won't need to wear a suit coat to eat it."

He smiled, but I felt the unintended prick of those words. I'd miscalculated. Badly.

"Do you want to go someplace else?" I said. "Not to eat, but maybe shopping? I have clothing and necessities for you at the house, but I'm sure there are other things—"

"What you have will be fine. I'll probably stay in for a few days and acclimatize."

"We can visit in town. Gabriel's aunt, Rose, would love to see you. Others, too. We can visit, or they can come by. Maybe I'll throw a dinner party."

He spoke with care. "I would love that in a few days, Liv, but for now, I just need a little time."

I understood what he was saying, but my heart still sank. He was finally out of prison, and now what did he want? Another set of four walls.

"Although," he said, "there is one place I'd like to go when you have time."

"Yes?" I said, a little too eagerly.

"I'd love to just go for a walk. A forest hike would be great, but even a stroll in the countryside would do. I've missed that."

"There's a good trail between here and Cainsville," I said. "We could go for a hike now. Or later, if you'd prefer."

"If it's on the way, now would be great."

TWO

OLIVIA

TODD MAY have suggested a hike to please me, but as soon as I pulled over at the unmarked trailhead, his eyes lit up. He was out of the car before I put it into park.

"Is it okay leaving Gabriel's car here?" he asked as he looked along the dirt road.

"It isn't a formal trail."

"Which is why I'm asking. I'm not even sure he'd appreciate you taking it down that gravel road."

"To Gabriel, an expensive car is merely a symbol of his success," I said as we walked into the woods. "That's not to say he doesn't enjoy it—if you think I drive too fast, don't ever ride with him. The car is an object, though. Repairable. Replaceable."

"Huh."

"Weird, I know. I'd never bring *my* car back here."

He smiled, and as we walked, his gait smoothed, strides lengthening, chin rising. At home in his surroundings. Comfortable in a way he wasn't in the city. This was his natural habitat, the one his blood called for.

Cŵn Annwn blood. The Wild Hunt was a branch of Welsh fae, though they'd broken off so long ago that they considered themselves a separate race. The true difference lay in their purpose. The Cŵn Annwn hunted murderers who'd escaped justice. Killers must have at least a trickle of fae blood in their veins to warrant the Hunt's justice. Even today, the Cŵn Annwn hunted in forests, which was why Todd felt the pull of the woods, as I did to a lesser extent. My own blood is both Cŵn Annwn and fae, the latter from my mother's side.

Seeing Todd stride into the forest reminded me that the local Cŵn Annwn wanted to speak to him. Their leader—Ioan—had brokered the original deal with my mother, and the Huntsmen had watched over Todd in prison. Ioan wanted to give Todd the opportunity to learn more about his heritage if he was interested.

I wasn't sure how Todd would feel about that. He would want to see Ricky, of course. Ricky Gallagher. My former lover. Current friend. Satan's Saints biker. Future gang leader. And, together with me, Ricky led the Hunt, in his role as an embodiment of Arawn, Lord of the Otherworld.

Ricky had been called off to Miami on business for his father. I hadn't told Todd that. I knew they were looking forward to seeing each other. I could suggest dinner next week with both Ioan and Ricky, but I bit my tongue. I'd already overwhelmed Todd with all the things I wanted to do, all the people who wanted to see him.

Let him breathe. Let him be.

When the path thinned, I hung back to let Todd get ahead as I resisted the urge to chatter like a hyperactive tour guide. Instead, I gave that tour in my head.

Oh, there's a cliff over there with a great view. Can you hear the river? At this time of year, it runs so strong I swear I can hear it in Cainsville. Hey, there's a butterfly and—

Todd stopped so short that I nearly crashed into him.

His head turned in a motion that reminded me of Ricky. A slow and deliberate swivel, tracking a sound as his eyes narrowed. A hunter's response. A predator's.

I didn't ask whether he'd seen or heard something. I knew he had. Or, like Ricky, it wasn't even so much hearing or seeing as sensing.

I followed Todd's gaze and saw trees. Yep, lots of trees. It was midafternoon with the sun hiding behind cloud cover that forecast April showers. Though, this deep in the forest, the trees alone blocked out enough light to send us into near dusk. I squinted into the shadows. Then I glanced at Todd. He wasn't squinting. He didn't need to. If I inherited any Cŵn Annwn night vision, it wasn't enough to be noticeable. His was, and he watched the forest intently.

Then he rolled his shoulders. Grunted softly. And my father returned in a quick and easy smile.

"Jumpy," he said. "I'll be like that for a while, so ignore it. Gotta adjust to a life where no one lurks around every corner, waiting to…"

He caught my expression and reached out to squeeze my shoulder. "Sorry, sweetheart. I shouldn't joke like that in front of you. I was fine in prison. Whatever you see on TV, it wasn't like that for me. It isn't like that for most guys, but I had it even easier. Ioan made sure of that. I had Keating's protection from the start, and I have a knack for getting myself out of trouble before it comes to blows. Even when it does…" He shrugged. "I was in decent shape when I went in, and I got better. Guys didn't really bother me. Not the guards and not the inmates."

To some extent, that would have been true. He'd had Keating, his Huntsman protector who'd infiltrated the guards. He'd also had his Cŵn Annwn charm, that quick smile and an aura of peace and infectious calm. Still, I knew he was downplaying his situation for me. Downplaying it a lot. He'd gone into prison when he'd been younger than me, a slightly built, good-looking young man. Also a convicted serial killer. I would like to think that the two things played off one another—that predators would back off when they heard what he was in for. My fear, though, was that the combination had compounded, and he'd had to deal with both the felons who thought him a very pretty boy and those who used his serial killer status as an excuse to go after him, a justifiable target for their rage.

"Liv?" he said. When I didn't respond, his voice firmed, and he said, "Eden?"

My old name got my attention, as always. He took hold of my chin and turned my gaze to his.

"I am fine," he said. "I can look after myself. It might not seem like it sometimes, but I can. If you ever doubt that, have Gabriel show you my early prison record. I held my own, and after a while, no one bothered me. I figured out how to play the game. I was fine."

I nodded. As he eased back, something caught his attention again. He shifted into that other Todd, and in seeing it, I took comfort. He *could* look after himself. He wasn't a child. Wasn't a lamb lost among the wolves.

I knew that for a fact. One of my own gifts is the ability to access memories. If I make physical contact while someone is actively recalling an event, I might tumble into that memory myself and experience it as they do. So I had seen what Todd did in a forest not unlike this one. He'd summoned the Cŵn Annwn by murdering a serial killer they could not catch. When Todd had seen what the man did, I'd felt my father's rage, and I knew he had a capacity for violence. A deep capacity. He just had no stomach for it. No craving, either.

This time, when Todd looked around, I inched forward and whispered, "You sense something?"

His nose crinkled in a way I knew well from Gabriel or Ricky or even myself when it came to any mention of our fae "gifts." We are uncomfortable with the idea that we have any sort of special power, as if we're laying claim to the kinds of abilities that belong in comic books.

"I thought I saw someone." He corrected that to, "Some*thing*," and then added, "Probably just an animal."

"You said some*one*."

That face again. "I don't know. It's gone now, whatever it was. Could have been a fellow hiker."

"We should still be careful."

"No one followed us, Liv. I checked. So did you. I saw you looking. Nobody realized we switched cars, so that isn't a journalist lurking in the forest. Even if it is, well, then he gets a lovely photo of me hiking."

"I—"

"There's no one here, Liv." He waved his arm at the forest. "Just my overactive imagination. Like I said, it'll take a while for me to get used to this." He slapped my back. "Let's go home. I've worked up an appetite, and that steak dinner is calling."

I lived in Cainsville, a very old, very insular town outside Chicago. Founded by Welsh fae—the Tylwyth Teg—fleeing the Old World. They'd built it as a refuge for themselves and their human descendants. I'd guess at least three-quarters of the residents have fae blood. To them, though, it's just a lovely little town where they grew up.

The kind of sleepy, old-fashioned village that most kids can't wait to escape, and then find themselves coming back to when they want to raise children of their own.

While my mother's family came from Cainsville, she didn't grow up there. I had only very distant family in town. Gabriel had more. His mother, Seanna, was in long-term care there, and the less said about her, the better. Gabriel's father, Patrick, was one of the fae. The relative he was close to was his great-aunt Rose, who lived around the corner from us.

When I pulled into the driveway, Todd whistled as he saw my place, a Queen Anne on an oversized lot, a picture-perfect house on a picture-perfect street.

"Now that's a house," Todd said. "You said it belonged to Pam's great-grandmother?"

I nodded. "Mom used to come here as a child. It's been empty for years. The elders sold it to me at a very reasonable price. A bribe for staying in Cainsville."

Todd got out and gazed up at the house. "I remember when Pam and I first looked for a place. She was pregnant, and I wanted something like this. Smaller, of course. And in much worse shape. A fixer-upper project for me. She wanted a modern home. Less work, she said, which is true, but when I said I didn't mind the work, she put her foot down. No old houses for us. I got the feeling they brought back…"

He looked up and down my street. "I was going to say bad memories, but I remember her talking about her great-grandmother, and those certainly didn't seem like bad memories."

"It's the town. She hated it here." I paused. "The fae."

He nodded in understanding. My mother's "gift" was the ability to see through glamours. To recognize fae. That might seem like a wondrous thing for a child, being able to see magic in the world. It wasn't, because she knew nothing of magic or fae. She only knew that she saw people who were not really people, and something in her gut said this was bad; they were dangerous; they were wrong. A survival instinct. Fae are not good fairies, here to help humankind. They aren't here to murder us all, either. They just don't really give a damn, and if we stand between them and a goal, they have little compunction about ending us.

As we headed for the front porch, the dark clouds finally made good on their threat, erupting in a sudden downpour that set us running. Gabriel pulled open the door before we reached it.

Once inside, Gabriel took the takeout bag with a murmur that he'd warm lunch while I showed my father around. The main floor tour was quick. Kitchen, dining room, parlor and a small room that we'd turned into a library.

I called it "my" house only out of habit. While Gabriel still had his condo in the city, we flowed between them, depending on our schedule. We also had a lakefront cottage that Gabriel got, so we'd have a place that was truly "ours." Because clearly, if dual residences were awkward, the solution was to buy a third. Problems of the young and wealthy.

Upstairs there were four bedrooms. Ours was the front corner one with the half gable. The other front bedroom used to be Gabriel's when he'd sleep over before we got together. After we became a couple, we reconfigured the upper level, because, well, we don't necessarily want guests sleeping right beside us, not with these thin, old walls. We'd converted Gabriel's old room into our en suite bathroom and dressing area. The guest room became the one that didn't share any walls with ours. The fourth bedroom was an office.

By the time I showed Todd his room, Gabriel had reheated dinner. We ate with small talk, comfortable enough. Afterward, Todd insisted on helping tidy, but then he wanted to retire to his room.

"I'll take some time to settle in," he said. "I'll probably go to bed early, too."

"Are you sure?" I said. "We could—"

A look from Gabriel stopped me.

"All right," I said. "If you change your mind, we're here. A movie, a board game, a drink…"

"I'll be fine," he said. "You guys enjoy your evening. I've got that new cell phone to figure out. Maybe I'll spend some time with the instructions guide."

"That'd be online," I said. "But I can download—"

He waved for me to stay where I was. "I'm probably too tired to tackle reading tonight, anyway." He paused. "Did I see a tub in the main bathroom?"

"Yes, but there's a better one off our room. A soaking tub with—"

His hand rose to stop me. "The one in the main bathroom is fine. It's a tub. I have *dreamed* of tubs."

"If you want—"

He cut me off again, this time with a kiss on my cheek. "The only thing I want is to take a long bath while my daughter relaxes with a glass of wine and stops fretting about me."

Once his footsteps sounded on the upstairs floor, I sagged into a kitchen chair.

"He's fine, Olivia," Gabriel said.

"I know."

He pulled out the chair beside mine and lowered himself into it. "You wanted today to be perfect. You're disappointed."

I shook my head.

"You are disappointed," he continued. "Not in his reaction, but in yourself. In failing to give what you consider the perfect homecoming."

I rubbed my face. "I just wanted…"

"He's happy. He's free, and he's—"

"Can we do something? I could use a distraction."

His brows arched.

"No," I said. "I'm a little stressed for that. Just…I don't know. I guess a glass of wine or…" I slumped. "I don't know."

Gabriel disappeared into the living room. At one time, I'd have taken this as a sign that he'd had enough of my crap. Enough dealing with my emotions. Because that was exactly what he used to do when faced with the prospect of handling an emotional outburst. It's what he still did if a client dared to get upset about the prospect of life in prison. Gabriel would suddenly get a call—*urgent, must answer*—and excuse himself.

After a while, if I was the one upset, he wouldn't just walk away. He'd flee. Having always avoided dealing with emotion—in others and himself—he had no idea how to handle it, even when he might want to. Of course, all I'd seen was that he walked away.

Now, when he left the room, I knew he'd be back. He was getting something. It just wouldn't occur to him to say so. He simply walked out.

He returned with a Scotch bottle in one hand and two tumblers in the other. As he walked, he deftly uncapped the bottle one-handed and poured a finger into each glass. Then he set one glass in front of me. Paused. Considered. Added another finger to mine and then put the bottle aside.

I smiled. "Better than wine."

"I thought so."

He tugged his tie off and laid it on the chair back before popping open his top button.

My smile lingered as I watched. He stopped after one open button. Hardly a striptease, yet in some ways, it was. Gabriel letting down his guard. Gabriel relaxing, as he couldn't do around anyone except me. The ice in his eyes melted, irises turning the pale blue of well-worn jeans, soft and familiar. He ran a hand through his wavy black hair, breaking the gel hold and letting it tumble over his widow's peak. At thirty-one, faint lines had already sprouted around his eyes and mouth, but it was definitely not a bad look for him. He had a broad face, harsh, with a strong nose and strong jaw, a face that would age well as it matured.

I lifted off my seat, leaned across the table and pressed my lips to his.

"Thank you," I said, "for today."

His lips parted, and he seemed ready to speak, to pursue my opening and talk about today and my father. Then he caught my eye, nodded again and sipped his Scotch.

"We have a new case," he said. "One you might find interesting."

I grinned and settled back in my seat. "Tell me about it."

THREE

OLIVIA

GABRIEL'S NEW case wasn't particularly urgent. It wouldn't even require more than routine investigative work. Telling me about it was only a distraction. A topic to discuss that took my mind off my father.

Todd came down a while later to ask a few questions about his cell phone. I suspected he just did that to please me—he wouldn't have any immediate need of it. The only people he'd call were me or Gabriel. His parents were dead. He had a half sister he didn't know well, and she'd cut ties after his arrest.

Growing up, Todd had plenty of friends, like-minded guys from that era, living in a small city, finishing high school and getting good-paying jobs in factories or the trades. While the others had reveled in their newfound freedom and disposable income, Todd had gotten married, moved to the city and had a child with serious medical needs. He no longer fit in with his old crowd, and he had no time to make new friends. Even if he had, I doubted they'd be anyone he could share more than an awkward catch-up beer with now.

As for my mother, I didn't know the status of their relationship, and I didn't want to ask. There was a bond there, an unbreakable one. Communication, naturally, had been difficult and sporadic. He hadn't asked to contact her since he'd been out. Nor had he mentioned going to see her. He might. If he did, I'd honor his wishes. I sure as hell wasn't going to suggest it, though. He might have forgiven her. I couldn't. I was my mother's daughter, and I'd carry my grudges to the bitter end.

Todd would get a job. He would move into his own place. He was eager for both, while also knowing that he needed to find his footing first. Get his driver's license. Upgrade his skills. Spend time in the world, acclimatizing. He hadn't even shopped for groceries in two decades. The most mundane experiences could be overwhelming to him. I'd read enough on reintegrating ex-cons to know this. I just hadn't really understood it until now.

After Todd went to bed, Gabriel and I did some paperwork at the dining room table. This was where we preferred to work, both of us on our laptops, rarely speaking but still together.

I was deep in online research when my cell phone revved. Ricky's ringtone. I motioned to Gabriel that I'd take it out back so he could work in peace. His mouth opened to tell me that wasn't necessary, but I slipped out to the deck before he could stop me.

"Hey," I said to Ricky. "How's Miami?"

"No hurricanes this time. Still hot. Still humid. It's getting better now that the sun's dropping, so I'm hanging out at the pool."

"Got your swim trunks on, catching some rays, getting a spring tan…"

"Nah. I'm just occupying a lounge chair. Fully clothed."

"You do realize you're disappointing every woman—and some guys—at that pool. At least take your T-shirt off."

He laughed. "It's all families here."

"So, they can still admire. Take your shirt off. That's an order, and my goodwill deed for the day."

He only laughed again, and I heard him gulp a drink.

"That better have an umbrella in it," I said.

"Actually, it does. I eyed the beer selection and decided I'd earned something stronger."

"Rough day?"

"Just long. Lots of negotiating. I won, so it's all good. And I hear you had a lovely lunch with your dad."

I snorted. "Gabriel told you?"

"Warned me."

"He also asked you to call, didn't he? I'm not talking to him about it, so he's called in the reinforcements and asked for help."

"Gabriel ask for help? Never. He simply let me know how it went in case I should wish to speak to you this evening, and if I did, he might suggest that a call would be best, as it has been a long day for you, and texting would be onerous. Also, you may be busy tomorrow, so tonight is preferable."

I laughed again, easing onto a deck chair. "Well, thank you for correctly deciphering his SOS signal. Yes, I had a rough day. Yes, I'm not talking to him about it, but only because I don't need to discuss it. I expected too much. I made mistakes. I feel bad. I'll get over it."

"So I prepared a big speech, and now I don't get a chance to use it? Screw that. You're stuck with it."

I stretched out on the chair. "Will it include any analogies?"

"Only bad ones. Long, rambling, ultimately pointless personal stories that are intended to make an analogy and totally miss the mark. That's the only kind I do."

"Can't wait."

"Good. Now, first, establishing my credentials, I believe I'm the person in your life best suited to discuss your father's release with you, having some experience with the subject matter."

"Being released from prison?"

"Never. I lead a blameless life. And even if I didn't, I have an awesome lawyer. However, I may have friends who have spent time in jail."

"Because your awesome lawyer failed?"

"Yeah, you go inside and tell him that. See where you spend the night. Awesome lawyer is awesome, but even he can't save us from ourselves. So I've known guys who've been released. The difference is that they were only away for a year or two. Your dad got locked up when he was my age. Yeah, you know that. But I can't help imagining it. Go to prison at my age. Get out when I'm double that. You've thought about this. I know you have. It's just...I'm not sure we can really comprehend it."

"I'm trying."

"I know, but..." He trailed off. "Should I shut up now?"

"No."

"I'm not saying you need to try harder. That isn't possible. If Gabriel is worried—okay, yeah, he *is* worried, so forget *if.* He's worried that you're trying too hard. The truth, Liv, is that we *can't* imagine what this is like for Todd. The thing is..." He exhaled. "Did I ever tell you about the dog I got when I was ten?"

"No."

"There's a reason for that. So, I'm ten, and my dad wants to buy this auto-body shop. While he's negotiating the price, I wander around back and find this dog chained to the building. Five-foot chain. No shelter. Filthy bowls. The dog's thin and mangy. I don't touch it, of course. I know better. But I show my dad, and I beg him to help. He talks to the shop owner. Guy bought the mutt as a guard dog, but it didn't work out, so he kept it tied behind the shop. Dad buys the dog from him. I'm thrilled. I'm going to nurse it back to health and give it the most amazing doggie life ever, and it'll be my best friend and love me forever."

"Didn't work out that way, did it?"

"Hell, no. That dog had spent its life behind an auto-body shop, on a five-foot chain. No one walked it. No one petted it. No one said a kind word to it. So it wanted nothing to do with this kid who kept shoving toys at it and throwing balls for it and bringing it treats. Within a week, the dog bit me hard enough I needed stitches. It went to live with one of the guys in the club who didn't have kids and used to foster shelter dogs." A pause. "Shit. I just compared your dad to a half-crazed mutt that nearly bit my hand off. Great…"

I shifted the phone to my other ear. "No, don't worry. I get it."

"Whew."

"You're telling me how your early experience with that dog prepared you for nursing Lloergan back into a healthy, trusting cŵn."

He paused. "Uh…"

I laughed. "Just kidding, though I'm sure it helped with her. You're reminding me that my father has spent twenty years like that dog, tied to his cell, with minimal social interaction. You were the kid eager to save a neglected dog. I'm the one eager to fix my father's ruined life. He needs time to heal and adjust."

"Which you know."

"But I need more reminders. Okay, point taken. I'll back off. Now, speaking of Lloe, did Ioan tell you what she got into while you were gone?"

"No…"

"Excellent. You'll love this one. So Ioan texted me yesterday. Apparently, your cŵn…"

FOUR

GABRIEL

GABRIEL LAY on his back, listening to the sound of Olivia not sleeping. She'd seemed fine after talking to Ricky. She'd come into the house with a genuine smile on her lips and a lightness in her step and a calm in her eyes. At one time, that would have been a knife in his gut. A reminder of the bond she shared with Ricky. A reminder of what he had been to her, and a reminder that she'd been happy with him.

Happy with Ricky. Happier with Gabriel. That's what Olivia would say, and he knew that was true. She loved Ricky. Present tense, not past. But that love could be fully expressed in friendship. She said once it should have always been friendship, and it only became more because that seemed natural for an unattached man and woman. Which might be true, and yet, when Gabriel considered the matter, detached from emotion and jealousy, he was glad it had gone beyond friendship. That question had been answered, that temptation removed. Ricky and Olivia knew that as happy as they'd been together, their relationship had been static, lacking a future.

It was Gabriel who got half her closet. It was Gabriel who shared a bed with her *every* night. And it was Gabriel who wore her ring, a joke that was not really a joke, an old-fashioned promise ring she'd given him as a declaration that this was where she wanted to be and who she wanted to be with. When she was ready, he would replace her own promise ring with an engagement one, and he had no doubt she'd accept it.

With that, he knew his place in Olivia's life, and he knew Ricky's, and so the knife no longer twisted when Ricky lifted her mood after Gabriel could not. Instead, he saw Ricky as a tool in his kit for making Olivia happy. Yes, perhaps "tool" was unfair. Gabriel respected Ricky, liked him, even considered him a friend. What he meant was that he accepted that Ricky had a talent for calming and centering Olivia in a way Gabriel could not.

As they settled into bed, though, the effect of Ricky's call had worn off, and Olivia's mind had nothing to do but fret. Lying on his back beside her felt insensitive. Yet when he'd turned toward her and laid a hand on her hip, she'd stiffened. It had only lasted a second before she gave him a rueful smile and a "maybe tomorrow night," as if he'd been initiating sex. That could have stung. Except...

Except it was not untrue. That was how their nights went. Unless one or the other fell into bed exhausted, they had sex. Made love, curled up together and fell into happy, satisfied sleep.

It wasn't as if Gabriel had expected sex after her rough day. He never *expected* it, any more than she did. What he'd thought, instead, was that sex could be a way to distract her. He'd please her, and then she'd fall into that happy, satisfied sleep.

Her tensing had told him he'd made the wrong move. So now he needed to make the right one. Reach out and pull her to him and make it very clear that nothing more would be happening tonight.

Skip the lovemaking. Move straight to the cuddling. Hold her and kiss her and tell her it'd be all right. Let her know he was thinking of her, and that she was loved.

Simple. So perfectly simple. So why the hell was he lying on his back, staring at the dark ceiling, listening to her breathe?

Because he wasn't quite certain how to proceed.

Well, first you turn to actually face her...

What if he made it worse? He could tell her he didn't want sex, but she might still think he was hopeful. Also, if he cuddled her, his physical response might belie his words. Would she be angry? Offended? What if his hands accidentally slid where they shouldn't? Would she shove him away? Stalk out and sleep downstairs? The last thing she needed right now was an insensitive clod wheedling for sex when he knew she wasn't in the mood.

He shouldn't need to worry about this. They'd been together over a year. There should have been plenty of cuddling that didn't follow lovemaking or lead to it.

Except there wasn't.

Blame a collision of circumstances. First, Olivia had an appetite for sex. A deep appetite. He remembered Rose warning him about that, early on, when she suspected Gabriel might be withdrawing his friendship from Olivia because she'd begun sleeping with Ricky.

"If it doesn't go well with Ricky, she'll find someone else. Someone you'll like and respect a whole lot less than him. Someone who will be a hell of a lot less understanding about how much time she spends with you. Olivia appreciates men."

That was Rose's way of saying Olivia liked sex. And Gabriel had absolutely no problem with that.

He used to worry that he wouldn't live up to Ricky. For Gabriel, sex had always been efficient—he'd get it quickly and then leave quickly, hoping the combination would discourage women from calling him the next day. He'd considered his own appetite perfunctory, as it was in most things. With Olivia, he'd realized he had only needed a partner he cared for, someone he could relax with and enjoy. Someone he *wanted* to please.

The issues with his pre-Olivia sex life arose from the second part of the "collision of circumstance." Gabriel's childhood had been devoid of physical affection. There'd been none from his mother, and Rose had shown her affection with attention and kindness and love, but she was not the hugging type, which meant that he grew up the same, to the point where he avoided physical contact. The only exception was Olivia, and he didn't merely tolerate her touch—he welcomed it, craved it.

If asked before today, he'd have said he and Olivia had a very physically affectionate relationship. Then he'd felt her jump when he'd kissed her head at the restaurant. Not dismayed. Merely surprised. He rarely did that at all, let alone in public. Kissing and hugging were for sex—a precursor or an aftermath or part of the act itself. She'd peck his cheek in greeting or leaving, or she'd put one arm around him in a quick embrace. His physical affection came through simple touches, as it had even before they began dating. A hand on her back. A squeeze of her arm. His fingers on hers.

Turn to face her, and touch her hip again, and tell her you mean nothing by it, and then hold her.

That's all. Just hold her.

He took a deep breath and began to flip over—

Olivia's head shot up, and he froze, the words on his lips. *I was just—*

"Did you see that?" she said, pushing up from her pillow.

He was ready to ask what she'd seen. An omen, perhaps? Instead, he followed her gaze to the security panel. The elders had hated him installing that—it suggested they could not keep their Matilda safe. Gabriel didn't care. The Tylwyth Teg had made mistakes before, and whatever magical wards they used, he trusted locks and alarms more.

The panel showed green, all the doors closed, the house secured.

"Hmm?" he said.

"The lights flickered," she said. "It was disarmed and rearmed."

That had him out of bed in a blink. He faced the door, tense and listening. Then he remembered they had a guest.

"Your father?" he said. "Stepping out?"

She shook her head. "I didn't get a chance to show him the system."

The only other person with the code was Ricky. Even if he'd flown back to help Olivia in a crisis—which he'd been known to do—the front door had double deadbolts, one with a key lock and a second that could only be secured from inside.

Olivia took her gun from the bedside table. It wasn't kept in a lockbox. Rather, Gabriel had ordered a nightstand specially made with a secret compartment. Otherwise, he'd be haunted by visions of her sleeping alone while he worked late, and an intruder finding it and using it against her.

Gabriel himself did not carry weapons. That wasn't ego so much as habit. His size kept most threats at bay. His fists did the rest. Which wasn't to say he didn't own weapons—he kept them in his condo, secreted away, a leftover security blanket from a youth spent on the streets.

He strode barefoot from the bedroom, wearing only sweatpants, a concession to having a guest in the house. Behind him, Olivia pulled on a silk wrapper as he padded down the hall. Todd's door was closed, as it had been since he retired.

Gabriel took the stairs with care. The fourth one would squeak, so he skipped it. One near the base unexpectedly chirped under his weight. He stopped and listened.

Gabriel's fae blood gave him only one special ability: a preternatural sixth sense for trouble. He paused, and he looked, and he listened, but he sensed nothing.

At the bottom of the stairs, Olivia moved past him. As always, he resisted the urge to tug her behind him where she'd be safe. Pointless, really. One, she had the gun. Two, danger was equally likely to come from behind, and he'd rather she was in front, where he could see her.

Moonlight flooded through the rear patio doors. They'd never bought blinds. This wasn't the sort of neighborhood where people spied on their neighbors, even for idle amusement. That might have something to do with shockingly high fines for trespassing, peeping or any other invasions of privacy. The last thing the fae wanted was a bored neighbor peering through his binoculars when they relaxed at home and shed their glamours.

Olivia had her gun in hand but lowered. After investigating the case of a husband shot by his wife as an intruder, she didn't even walk around with the safety off.

As she glanced back at him, something moved beyond the patio doors. Gabriel tensed, ready to grab Olivia at the first sign of a rising gun barrel. Instead, he saw only a figure leaning over the railing, staring into the yard. When the figure's hand moved, Gabriel tensed again as the man lifted…

A beer bottle. He raised the bottle to his lips, and Gabriel noticed the man's stature and light hair.

"Todd," he murmured.

Olivia was already jogging to the door. She flung it open so fast Todd jumped. Then he saw the gun in her hand, and his own hands shot up, fumbling the bottle.

"Sorry." Olivia set the gun on the counter before she stepped out. "I saw the system disarm and rearm, and I hadn't given you the code."

"Sure you did, sweetheart. The code plus very explicit instructions. It's in that huge binder upstairs, along with everything I need to know about the house. How to operate the coffee maker, the microwave, the shower…I didn't find instructions for the toilet, but I think I've got it figured out. Flush *after* using. Right?"

"Okay, I might have gone a little overboard. I just wanted you to be comfortable here."

"I know, and I am." He lifted his bottle. "Got a beer. Figured out the alarm. Snuck off to enjoy the evening. If—"

Todd gave a start as a black shape leapt onto the railing. The cat settled in and fixed its gaze on him.

"TC?" Todd asked.

Olivia nodded. "Yep."

"He…has a very intense stare."

"He's trying to figure out who you are, why you're here and, most importantly, whether you can open a tuna can." She paused. "Nope, that's a lie. He's really only interested in the last part."

"Can I pet him?"

"You can try."

Todd held the cat's unblinking stare. "And risk a bloody arm?"

"He doesn't scratch or bite. He might enjoy being petted, or he might look at you like you're a peasant daring to touch nobility. Depends on his mood."

"He's a fae cat, right?"

"He's a matagot. In lore, they give golden coins. It's a scam. All *he* gives are those looks. He's been around a long time, though. He used to hang out with Mom when she visited here."

"And now he's yours."

"He's not really anybody's. He only deigns to accept my food." She motioned at the open door. "Your dinner awaits, sir."

TC hopped down and regally strode into the kitchen.

"We'll leave you be," Olivia said to Todd.

"You're welcome to join me. It's a nice night." He looked over her shoulder. "You, too, Gabriel. Grab a beer and come out. Just leave any weapons on the counter, please."

"Gabriel doesn't carry weapons," Olivia said.

"Because Gabriel *is* a weapon." Todd smiled at him. "I've seen you in court. Pretty sure you can talk your way out of anything."

"Usually," Olivia said as she tossed Gabriel a grin. "But sometimes he uses his fists instead. More satisfying. I'll sit out for a few minutes. I'm not tired. And you...?"

Gabriel shook his head. "I'll go back to bed."

She watched him a moment, making sure he was all right with that. He was. It saved him from making a mistake trying to comfort her. A coward's move, perhaps, but Gabriel hated making mistakes.

He started to withdraw. Stopped. Moved forward and kissed the top of her head, and then headed back upstairs.

FIVE

OLIVIA

I WAS up early the next morning to make breakfast, as much for Gabriel as for my father. Gabriel was going into work while I stayed home with Todd. As we ate, Todd said he'd be fine by himself.

"I've got my binder," he said. "I can operate all the appliances, and I'm sure Gabriel needs you in the office."

Gabriel glanced at me. Not urging me to come in—we'd cleared my investigative desk. He was just checking in case I wanted the excuse.

"I'll work from home today and tomorrow," I said. "I might go in Thursday."

Todd insisted on cleaning up after we ate, and as Gabriel finished getting ready, I took my laptop into the dining room. Or I did for two minutes before I hefted it under my arm, stalked upstairs and shoved it onto the bathroom counter while Gabriel adjusted his tie.

"Fix it," I said.

His brows lifted. "I believe you are mistaking me for a computer technician. If you require support, the number is in our contact list."

"The number I need is in your *personal* contact list. Lydia's grandson."

"You know that I prefer to be the point of contact for Bryant. In the event that anything I should ask him to do skirts the borders of legality, I don't want any link between him and you."

"You're going to play this all the way, aren't you?"

"I have no idea what you're talking about, Olivia." He plastered a stray curl back in place, gave his reflection a cursory glance and headed into the bedroom. "Should you decide to leave Todd to his own devices and drive into the city, I am free for lunch today."

"I need to look out for him."

"He is a grown man, and this house is as secure as humanly possible. If you are truly concerned, ask Veronica to come over. She'd like to meet him, and she is the elder least likely to cause him any discomfort. In fact, I'd suggest you introduce them even if you don't wish to join me for—"

"For a brilliant man, you are so very good at playing dumb. It's an art form with you."

He took his suit jacket from the closet. "It is not 'playing dumb.' It is feigning innocence. I have a lifetime of experience at it. However, in this case, I really do not know—"

"You hacked my computer and blocked me from searching on my father's name."

"That would be wrong."

"Yep, which is not a denial."

"Perhaps you are mistaken, and there is simply nothing online about your father's release from prison."

I stepped in front of him as he moved for the hall. A wave of my hand sent him back into our room with a deep, put-upon sigh.

I closed the door behind us so Todd couldn't overhear. "Thanks to you, we got out of the prison without a battalion of reporters waiting, because they all expected him to be released today. I appreciate that. However, I screwed up, and we were spotted at that restaurant, and someone notified the media. They swarmed. And yet, apparently, they decided the release of Chicago's most notorious serial killer didn't warrant even a mention in today's papers."

"It is rather dull news."

"Do you want to come home tonight? Because I know how to change the security codes."

"That would only bring the local police, which would be terribly embarrassing for you."

"I can change the locks."

"I can pick them."

"Not the single-side deadbolt."

He sighed again and backed to sit on the bed. "You don't need to read those articles, Olivia."

"Yes, I do. I need to know if there are any serious threats. We've discussed this, and you know it's plausible. What if, online, people start talking about doing something to him, but—whoops—you blocked me from seeing that site."

"I will be monitoring for legitimate threats."

I opened my mouth to argue. It took me a moment to come up with something. "Okay, but I know there's going to be bullshit on there. It won't bother me. I've gone through it for years myself."

"As have I. The difference, Olivia, is that if the vitriol is directed at ourselves, we don't care. The worse people say about me online, the more clients I get. It's free advertising. As for what they've said about you, it rolls off you. I understand that. Here's the difference. When I first met you, and you were being maligned online for being the daughter of convicted serial killers, I didn't care. It wasn't my concern, and I barely knew you. As I got to know you, that changed. It bothered me. Then it infuriated me. Then it enraged me. It was unfair. You'd done nothing wrong, and to have people saying these things about you was unconscionable. That is how you will feel seeing anything about Todd. Infuriated and enraged. And what can you do about that? Absolutely nothing."

I didn't answer, just stood there, in front of the bedroom door.

He took out his cell phone and punched a few keys. Then he turned it to me. On the page was an article about Todd's release. He'd scrolled down to the comment section. I took one look. Then I handed the phone back.

"I don't like being coddled," I said.

"Have I ever done such a thing?" He slipped the phone into his pocket. "Reading those comments can do you no good, and it's hardly a mark of character to do so. It will only cloud your mind and upset you. Focus on work. Perhaps join me for lunch, but I'll understand if you choose not to. Invite Veronica or Rose to tea, instead. If I find any credible threats online, I will let you know. I do not expect to. People can be small and hateful, and those comments are simply an expression of that."

"I know." I opened the door. "I won't say thank you for blocking my searches. I'd rather you asked first. But I know why you did it, and you're right. I don't need that."

⤻

KNOWING Gabriel was right did not keep me from fussing. It didn't keep me from running a search on my phone an hour later. When I found that he hadn't tampered with that, I closed the browser. Gabriel had not forgotten I could run the search on my phone or my tablet. Blocking my laptop wasn't barring me from looking up mentions of my father. It was the equivalent of turning the knob lock and leaving the deadbolts unfastened.

I'm merely making the point that you ought not to open this door. You will not like what lies behind it, and there is no reason for you to open it.

He was right. And so, when I found that I *could* open that door if I really wanted to, I decided I did not.

I went for a walk with Todd, and I had a coffee with him, and then I worked as he poked about the backyard and gardens.

I didn't go into the city for lunch. It was a long drive, and I knew the only reason Gabriel suggested it was a subtle hint that I shouldn't hover like an overanxious parent. Again, he had a point, and I *would* drive in tomorrow. I let him know that with a text, and then I made lunch. Todd and I ate out back, and I talked about my plans for the garden and how we planned to add a conservatory when we had time to hire and supervise contractors.

Over lunch, I saw a magpie. Not that unusual…if you lived in the western half of the country. They were extremely rare here unless you were me. Unless you saw things that didn't exist.

One for sorrow…

That omen was nearly enough to send me running to my cell phone to google my father's name. Instead, I settled for typing a reminder for Gabriel to conduct the search…which I deleted unsent. He would not forget, no matter how busy he got, and the reminder made me seem like a fretful child. Which I kind of was right now, but I'd rather not broadcast that any louder than I already had.

I returned to work. Midafternoon, when I heard Todd in the kitchen, I popped my head around the corner.

"Break time?" I said. "I have cookies. Baked them myself, and they are actually edible."

"I'd love one," he said. "But I was going to suggest… There's a local diner, right? Within walking distance? I remember you worked at one before you started investigating for Gabriel, and I'm presuming it's nearby."

"It is."

"I also recall your mom said a diner here made old-fashioned milkshakes. Same place?"

I nodded. "New owners, but same milkshakes."

"Let's do that, then." When I hesitated, he said, "Unless you're busy."

"Not at all. I just thought you might want to take it slower, meeting people here. The diner is where the elders hang out. It could be…overwhelming."

"Is anyone likely to ask if I'd like virgin's blood with my milkshake?"

I smiled. "Definitely not. You're welcome here. The elders are happy to have you. They can just be a bit intrusive. They take their senior citizen glamours to heart. Bunch of old busybodies."

"I am fine with busybodies."

"Let me grab my wallet, then."

SIX

OLIVIA

TC FOLLOWED us to the diner. Of course, he didn't act like he was following us. He's a cat. He pretended he was just going in the same direction, trotting across lawns and then, if a car passed, stopping to clean a paw, feigning indifference.

"He watches out for you," Todd said.

"No, he's just curious. With a new person in the house, he's wondering what's up. He's also hoping we're going to the diner. They give him cream."

"I thought cats weren't supposed to have cream."

"It's bad for them? Shhh. Don't tell him."

TC fixed me with a baleful look.

Todd laughed. "I think he understands you."

"Oh, I'm sure he does. It's a love-hate relationship. We love to hate each other, don't we, kitty?"

I swear TC rolled his eyes. He kept trotting along behind us, though, and I would get him his saucer of cream. I knew it wasn't ideal for his tummy, but it wasn't poison. For TC, it was like ice cream for a lactose-intolerant kid—it tasted too good for him to give up.

Cats weren't the only curious ones around, either. We passed a few people out walking dogs, and while they only gave us a cheerful "hello," I felt gazes following after us. When we headed down Rowan Street, I did not fail to see the curtains move on an adorable Victorian dollhouse across the road.

"Gabriel's aunt?" Todd asked.

"You see her?"

"No, but I see the sign in the window. *Rosalyn Z. Razvan, Take Charge of Your Future.* I'm guessing she's the only local psychic."

"She is."

I raised my hand as we passed, but Rose had already moved away, dealing with a client. She'd peeked out to see whether we were coming to her door. I knew better during office hours.

"Not even going to stop and say hello, are you?" a voice called from my other side.

"Hello, Grace," I called back. "Lovely day for a stroll."

"Get your ass over here, girl, and introduce me—"

"Love to. Can't. Feel free to get *your* ass off that front stoop, come to the diner and say hello."

Todd shot me a look of surprise and mild horror, that I should speak that way to a wizened old lady, sitting on her front stoop.

"She's not human," I said. "That's Grace. One of the elders. She's really a troll."

"I heard that," she called.

I paused to look back at her as I shaded my eyes. "Whoops. Sorry. Not a troll. *Are* there trolls?"

She glowered at me.

"She acts like one," I continued to Todd. "Guarding the front porch, there. She's the landlord. That's where I used to live. It's the only rental property in town, and trust me—you don't want to move in there. *Infested* with fae."

Grace snorted. "Better than being infested with humans. We've got one of those I'd like exterminated."

Todd looked at me, but I only shook my head and continued on. She meant Seanna—Gabriel's mother—but there was no need to explain to Todd. It was, however, another reason why Todd couldn't live there. I wasn't letting anyone I cared about near Seanna Walsh.

We cut through the passage beside Grace's building. I showed Todd the tiny park with its chimera fence. I did not show him the gargoyle hidden behind it. That was Gabriel's gargoyle, cast in his childhood likeness after he won the annual May Day contest to find all the town's gargoyles. Such a scavenger hunt might sound easy enough…except the gargoyles were sprinkled with pixie dust, appearing and disappearing, depending on the day, the season, the lighting, and so on. No child has found them all since Gabriel. I've only gotten two-thirds.

TC left us at the diner and began cleaning himself, as if expecting nothing. I pushed open the door, and there were exactly two seconds of dead silence, followed by a sudden bustle of movement and conversation, as everyone jumped to cover the fact they'd gone quiet.

I counted five elders, seated at three tables. All of them motioned for us to join them. Choosing was a political minefield; one I traversed with relish because the mines I set off didn't touch me at all. I was Matilda. Mallt-y-Dydd. Matilda of the Day. Matilda of the Tylwyth Teg. The living embodiment of the original, my very distant ancestor whose memories and gifts I held. As long as I lived in Cainsville, I granted the fae power by my very presence. I fed the local ley lines, which cleansed the elements—air and water and earth—that fed the fae's own powers. Of course, I'd be even more useful if they could claim my full favor, but I embraced both sides of Matilda, also helping the Cŵn Annwn as Mallt-y-Nos, Matilda of the Night, Matilda of the Hunt.

Even if I came to the diner alone, they'd vie for my attention. They'd do the same with Gabriel, as the embodiment of Gwynn ap Nudd, legendary king of the fae. We were as close to royalty as you could get, and we exploited that to our full benefit. We were fae—they expected no less of us.

My first choice would be Veronica, my personal favorite and someone I'd gladly dine with, politics aside. Yet of the five fae there, only one was part of the inner group. He sat by himself, as always. He was also the only elder who didn't look like a senior citizen. His glamour placed him close to my age. With longish dark hair, a sharp triangular face, and a fashionable amount of beard scruff, he looked like the stereotypical coffee-shop hipster working on his great American novel. He even sat in the front corner—the best seat in the house—typing on his laptop.

I could snub Patrick. I would, too, if I had cause, and God knows, he almost always gave me cause. Being honest, though, if I had to choose the elder after Veronica whose company I enjoyed most, it would be Patrick. I'd just never tell him that.

I didn't actually sit down with him. That'd be too obvious. Instead, I headed for the table behind his, but as we passed, I paused as if ready to introduce Todd. Patrick lifted his empty coffee mug. Patrick is a bòcan. Do good deeds for him, and he repays them, just as quickly as he repays bad ones. If I wanted to curry favor, I'd have walked in and filled that mug without him asking. When he lifted it today, I arched my brows and continued walking.

He caught my arm. "I'm joking," he said and set the mug down.

When he got to his feet, I tensed and calculated our quid pro quo balance, in case I'd unexpectedly tipped it out of my favor, and he was about to shun me by leaving. Instead, he extended a hand to Todd. This would, in any other circumstance, be the obvious reason for rising—to greet a newcomer. Yet fae don't do that, not in Cainsville.

"Patrick," he said as he shook Todd's hand. Then he even tugged over a chair from the next table. It seemed like the polite move, but I knew what he was really doing—making it harder for me to keep walking to another table.

I lowered myself to the new chair and let Todd take the other. The server hurried over, and we placed our order. When she was gone, I glanced about the diner. There was only one table of human patrons—Dr. Webster and her wife—and they were in the opposite corner. Safe enough.

"Patrick is Gabriel's father," I said.

Todd knew Gabriel's father was fae, so he only said, "Ah," and nodded, not the least perplexed by the fact that Patrick looked younger than his son.

"He's a hobgoblin," I said.

Patrick sighed. "Is that how you're going to start introducing us, Liv?"

"Sorry." I looked at Todd. "He prefers bòcan. Hobgoblin sounds like an ugly little green man, which he's not. Even without his glamour, he's full-sized."

I got a glare from Patrick for that. He was sensitive about his non-glamour shape. Most fae looked like supermodel versions of humans—tall, lithe and attractive with a faint glow that only added to their beauty. Patrick's was one of the least conventional.

It was what humans would associate with the "green man" of folklore, which made sense since some of that lore also referred to the green men as hobgoblins. Humans do get it right some of the time.

"What I meant," Patrick said, "is introducing us as our fae type. Doesn't that strike you as a tad racist, Liv?"

"Not at all. Forewarned is forearmed." I looked at Todd. "Hobgoblins—or bòcan—are what you might call karma fae. Do unto them as you'd have them do unto you."

"A fact which your daughter would do well to bear in mind," Patrick murmured to Todd.

"I'm sure Liv has this under control," Todd said, as he took his milkshake from the server.

Patrick only grumbled under his breath. It was a good-natured grumble, though, and Todd scored a point with that one. Patrick might claim to like sycophants, but he had no patience with them. Anyone who kowtowed to him earned only his disdain and, worse, bored him.

I took the saucer of cream out for TC. When I returned, Patrick was saying to Todd, "So how's life on the outside?"

"Better than life on the inside."

"I can imagine." Patrick shut his laptop and pushed it aside. "Which reminds me, at some point, I'd love to talk to you, as a reference." He gave me a quick look. "Not now. Whenever is convenient. I have a character in my new novel that spent ten years in prison, and I would love a…" He pursed his lips. "Normally, I'd say 'professional opinion,' but that seems wrong here."

Todd laughed softly. "I believe I do qualify as a professional convict. It's the only thing I *am* an expert in these days. So no offense taken. I'd be happy to read it over. You're writing a book?"

"He's written a lot of them," I said. "Even published some."

"You're a novelist?" Todd perked up. "Liv never mentioned that. What do you write?"

"Paranormal romance," I said. "Not your cup of tea, I'm sure."

"I've read those. Paranormal romance. Historical romance. Not big on contemporary romance, but I like the others." He caught my look. "Are you *judging* me for reading romance?"

"Yep, she's totally judging you," Patrick said. "Our Liv is something of a literary snob."

I wasn't. I just played the part to needle Patrick. I'd actually read about half of his books. I liked them, in spite of myself. Not that I told him how many I'd read. I doled out my praise as needed. Every six months or so, I'd say, "Oh, I read another one of yours. It was pretty good." That bought me more goodwill than a hundred refills of his coffee mug. If I admitted I'd read more, it'd dilute the effect.

"I like romance," I said. "Romantic suspense is more my style, but I read as much of that as I do mystery, and I expect a romantic subplot in my mysteries and thrillers. I just didn't think it'd be your thing."

"Because I'm a guy," Todd said. "Sexist."

"Incredibly sexist," Patrick said. "We're disappointed in you, Liv."

"I'm not saying guys wouldn't enjoy romance. They just don't usually pick it up."

"They do if they're in prison," Todd said. "You read what's on the shelf. Romance is one of the most popular genres, and I don't just mean the ones with the hot stuff. I like paranormal romance. It was a very welcome break from my reality." He glanced at Patrick. "Is that what this new book is?"

"No. The market for those is cooling, and I'm ready to move on. It was fun, but it's time for a change. My new one is what I'd call gothic mystery, contemporary, with a—"

A siren wailed outside. My head shot up. Patrick's brow furrowed, and everyone in the diner turned toward the sound with a frown.

"Is that a police siren?" Patrick said.

It very clearly was, but I understood his confusion. We don't hear police sirens in Cainsville. Local crime was nearly nonexistent. Ironic, given that Cainsville was home to the Walshes. Let's just say that despite the fact that he was a lawyer known for his "creative" defense strategies, Gabriel was actually the *white* sheep of the Walsh family. His family wasn't alone in its loose adherence to ethics. Cainsville was a town full of fae-blood humans.

Yet the Walshes—and presumably others—had a strict code when it came to their criminal endeavors. Don't shit in your backyard. It wasn't about avoiding prosecution. It was a recognition—equally fae in nature—that you don't cheat those you care about. You don't blackmail family. You don't con friends. You don't pickpocket neighbors. The outside world was fair game. But not here. Never here.

While there was little need for a police department, of course we had one. And if we saw one of the two local PD cars speeding up in our rearview mirror, we pulled over. No sirens or lights required.

So hearing that noise, everyone frowned in confusion. As the sound drew closer, I leaned backward to look out the window, and sure enough, a police car ripped along Main Street, lights flashing.

On the sidewalk, a trio of preschoolers turned to gape. One little girl clapped and bounced, as if it were a surprise parade. Her sitter—an elder—put a hand on her shoulder and quickly steered the children down the passage to the park.

The state police car pulled up in front of the diner. That was when I noticed Todd, his face pale, hand clasped tight around his milkshake glass.

"Dad?" I said.

He shot me a smile, but it was his reflexive one, his eyes empty. "Hmm?"

I wanted to say, "It's okay," or "They're not here for you," but that would be like reassuring an elderly parent succumbing to dementia. He wasn't honestly thinking those sirens were for him. He knew better. The response was as reflexive as that smile. It would remind him of his arrest.

No, they hadn't used sirens when they arrested him. I remembered the front door crashing in, men with guns storming through. Monsters, I'd thought at the time. Armed monsters in black dragging my parents away forever.

I squeezed my eyes shut and shuddered.

All better now. He's here. It wasn't *forever.*

That look on my father's face wasn't bad memories. It was current fear. Irrational but understandable. The fear that this was all a mistake. That they would find some loophole to drag him back to prison. He knew that wouldn't happen, but hearing these sirens would still twist his stomach.

The doors opened. Todd lifted his milkshake and took a long drink, his gaze straight ahead.

"Dr. Webster?" the first officer through the door called.

My father relaxed. I did, too, because, yes, I knew the courts couldn't overturn his release, but that didn't keep me from having nightmares about that exact scenario.

The young officer spotted the doctor in the back corner, and he hurried over. When he spoke to her, his voice resonated through the silent diner.

"We couldn't reach you," the officer said. "You're the local coroner, right?"

She rose. "Yes, of course." She checked her cell phone and winced. "Sorry. I had it on vibrate. Is there a problem?"

"We have a body a few miles outside town. Our coroner is off today, and we can't reach him. We were told to come get you."

Dr. Webster picked up her jacket and purse. "I'll need to get my bag. I can meet you there."

"Better wear boots. Body's back in the woods. Guy's been there a while."

She paused. "I know there's a Native American burial ground in the area. If it's possible the body came from there, you'll need to make more calls, and while I can attend, I shouldn't touch the body."

"Nah, it's not *that* old. Maybe twenty years. Looks like murder. That or an animal attack. Vicious, either way."

At a throat clearing from Dr. Webster's wife, both the doctor and the officer stopped and looked around, realizing they were broadcasting to an audience...who might not want the gory details with their afternoon tea.

I glanced at Todd, but he was fussing with his new phone, as if paying no attention to the scene unfolding. Not wanting to look over, I suspected, in case he was recognized.

The officer left. As Dr. Webster crossed the restaurant, she suddenly picked up speed, hurrying to the door and flinging it open.

"You didn't tell me where it was," she called after the officer.

"Oh, right," the reply came. "Off Willow Creek Road. Down near the end. You'll see the cars."

Willow Creek? Did he say...?

Yes, but I must be misremembering. That couldn't be...

I glanced at Todd. His head had jerked up, blood draining from his face.

Willow Creek Road. A long-buried corpse found in the forest, with signs of a brutal attack.

Twenty-four years ago, my father had murdered serial killer Greg Kirkman…in the forest off Willow Creek Road.

SEVEN

OLIVIA

THE BODY found could not be Greg Kirkman. The sheer coincidence made it impossible—one day after Todd was acquitted and released, the body of his one actual victim turns up? I had just been thinking about my anxiety dreams, and that was what this seemed like: the manifestation of my nightmare. The one way Todd could actually end up back in jail. That should mean I was fast asleep in bed, and any moment now, Gabriel would rouse me, murmuring, "You're having a nightmare."

Gabriel did not wake me.

I wasn't asleep.

Therefore, it was coincidence. Some unrelated body had turned up in the same rough geographic area. The officer said it wasn't old enough to come from the nearby Native American burial site, but he was hardly an expert. Or it wasn't that old. A twenty-year-old corpse should have skeletonized by now.

Yet I couldn't help thinking of that omen.

One for sorrow…

I shook that off as Todd and I headed back to the house. We'd left right after the doctor, making our excuses and hurrying out. We hadn't said a word since. Then, as we walked down my road, I stopped suddenly and turned to Todd.

"The Cŵn Annwn took the body, right?" I said.

He nodded.

"So, it can't be him," I said. "He wasn't buried there."

"I don't know where they took him. They just said they'd look after it."

"We need to speak to Ioan."

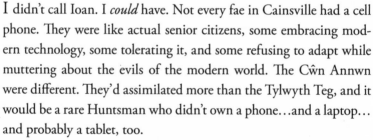

I didn't call Ioan. I *could* have. Not every fae in Cainsville had a cell phone. They were like actual senior citizens, some embracing modern technology, some tolerating it, and some refusing to adapt while muttering about the evils of the modern world. The Cŵn Annwn were different. They'd assimilated more than the Tylwyth Teg, and it would be a rare Huntsman who didn't own a phone…and a laptop… and probably a tablet, too.

This didn't seem a safe conversation to have by phone, though, so we were on our way to Ioan's place. I *did* call Gabriel. I didn't need to tell him what I was afraid of. As soon as I said what had been found and where, he knew my concern. I told him where we were going, and he said he'd get more details from his contacts in the state police.

Ioan lived northwest of the city, which was the same direction as Cainsville, but closer to Chicago, where he ran a security firm. The Cŵn Annwn made their living honestly. Their mission as Huntsmen was one of justice, and so their ethical standards were the polar opposite of normal fae. They went out of their way to emphasize that, to make the distinction clear. *We are not fae. Nope, not at all. We have standards.*

So it was both ironic and telling that Ioan's own son—Ricky's father—ran the Satan's Saints. For bikers, the club had a surprisingly strong ethical code. They wouldn't enter the sex trade. They avoided trouble with other gangs. They had zero tolerance for domestic violence. Yet they made at least half their money through the sale of guns and drugs. They weren't actual saints. In that, you could see the Cŵn Annwn mingling with older strains of fae blood. A strict code of rules and ethics...which could be broken, within those limits, to earn a living and protect themselves.

Before I left Cainsville, I'd texted Ioan to say I wanted to speak to him, and that it was a "matter of security," which wouldn't be incriminating, given what he did for a living. He'd prefer to discuss it at his house, so that's where we went. We were still coming down his rural road when I spotted his AMG ahead and the estate gates swinging open.

"That was fast," Todd said.

"I come by my speed-demon ways honestly," I said. "Cŵn Annwn blood."

He chuckled. "Can't say speeding was ever my problem, but I understand the appeal."

Despite his laugh, his body stayed tight, as it had been through the drive. Now his gaze followed that car as it disappeared into the drive.

"Have you met Ioan since that first time?" I asked.

"I don't think so," he said. "I can't say for sure."

I glanced over, frowning.

"When I saw him, he was a guy on a flaming horse," Todd said. "Green cloak. Hood pulled up. The only things visible under that hood were red eyes." A more strained chuckle. "I'm guessing that's not how he goes to work in the morning."

"Right. Sorry. I forgot you would have seen him as a Huntsman. He's a little less intimidating in person."

I turned into the drive. Ioan must have seen me down the road. He'd pulled into the garage at the top of the lane, leaving the door open as he came out to see me. Brenin—the lead cŵn—appeared from behind the garage.

I glanced at Todd, who hadn't noticed the man or the giant black hound. His gaze was on the manor house and sweeping lawns, like something out of an English novel. The lord's country abode.

"Nice," he said.

Yes, the Cŵn Annwn might be warriors of justice, but they hadn't taken a vow of poverty. I was about to comment when Todd noticed Ioan, still fifty feet away, walking from the top of the long drive.

"That's him, I take it?" Todd said. "He definitely looks like Ricky's grandfather."

"He does."

I climbed from the car, and Todd did the same. The man walking toward us was trim, fit and well built, in his early sixties, attractive, with an easy smile and easy stride. Confident, no hint of arrogance. He could *be* Ricky in forty years, age adding only self-possession and sophistication.

For the Cainsville elders, taking on the form of senior citizens was their way of hiding in plain sight. They take advantage of humans' ageism. We see a gray-haired and wrinkled person, and we don't pay them much attention, don't notice when, twenty years later, they still look the same.

Ioan wasn't that sort of senior citizen. He was the modern sort, still able to work ten hours a day running his own corporation, host a dinner party and then slip in a few holes of golf before bed. Or, in his case, go for a nice horseback ride and reap the souls of the damned. Same thing, really.

The local Cŵn Annwn had come up with their own way of hiding their longevity. In Ioan's office, there was a photo of his son, also named Ioan, who grew up with his mom in Florida and was now in grad school. In a few years, Ioan Senior would suffer a sudden and fatal heart attack, and his son would come to Chicago to take over the family business, under the direction of the board of directors. That board of directors? The other Huntsmen. And Ioan Junior? It would be Ioan, in a much younger glamour, which he'd age at a natural human rate and then repeat the whole process.

Ioan reached us and put his hand out, taking Todd's and then, as they were shaking hands, pulling him into a half embrace, his arm around my father's shoulders.

"I'm sorry," Ioan said, his voice low. "I'm so sorry."

Todd shook his head as they separated. "You didn't put me in there. Pam did it for both of us."

The expression that flickered over Ioan's face said he agreed with me—the situation wasn't that simple, my mother not that blameless—but the look vanished in the easy Cŵn Annwn smile my father shared.

Todd looked up as another man approached.

"Keating," he said to the Huntsman who'd infiltrated the prison guards to watch him. "Have you been celebrating your release, too? That wasn't how you wanted to spend twenty years, I'm sure."

"I got to go home at night." Keating shook Todd's hand. "I'm glad to be out, though, if it means you're out, too."

"And his real name is Trahaearn," I said.

Todd tried to pronounce that, and Trahaearn laughed and said, "You can stick with Keating."

"No, I'll get it. I just might mangle it a few times."

"Come inside," Ioan said. "I do believe it's cocktail hour. I'm not much of a bartender, but Trahaearn mixes an excellent martini. And Liv has seen my wine cellar. Anything in there is yours. It's a day for celebration."

"We didn't really come for a social visit," I said.

"I know, but unless it's urgent, I believe we can speak just as well over wine and a cheese tray."

I let Ioan make a fuss of our visit. He wasn't downplaying our emergency. He was easing the tension and welcoming Todd properly. I went along with it because it also conveyed the message to my father that I wasn't worried about the current situation. Nope, not at all. It was just an excuse to bring him to Ioan and settle this matter over cocktails.

Trahaearn went into the kitchen to prepare a snack. As he got that, I took Todd to the wine cellar, where we picked out a bottle.

As I came out of the cellar, Lloergan poked her shaggy head around the corner and fixed me with a reproachful stare. Then she withdrew, and her big paws padded away, as if she wasn't terribly interested in my arrival, since I hadn't even bothered to come see her.

"Lloe!" I called and hurried after her. "I totally forgot you were here." I set the bottle on a sideboard and dropped to my knees to hug her. "Sorry, baby."

She relaxed and nuzzled me as I petted her. Lloergan is Ricky's cŵn. She's smaller than Brenin but still as big as a Great Dane and as shaggy as a Newfoundland. Cŵn means "hound" in Welsh, Cŵn Annwn literally translating into "the hounds of the Otherworld." We use the term to refer to the Huntsmen, but technically, the *hounds* are the Cŵn Annwn. They are the black dog of folklore. The black shuck. The devil dog. The barghest. Whatever you wish to call them. In folklore, they are fetches—see one, and your soul is about to be fetched away to the afterlife. In truth, they do the fetching themselves. They bring down the Huntsmen's prey and send their souls to the Otherworld.

Ricky found Lloergan two years ago, as an abused and neglected hound who'd been forced into service for a rogue Huntsman. Lloergan's one milky eye had improved to the point where the damage was barely noticeable. She was missing an ear, but we'd treated the scar tissue and restored most of her hearing. While her health had improved significantly, the mental and emotional damage took longer, which was why I was so quick to shower her in affection when she thought I'd snubbed her. Having Ricky away on business already left her feeling abandoned.

I turned to Todd as I kept petting the cŵn. "This is Lloergan. Or Lloe. She's Ricky's hound. His cŵn. The one I've mentioned."

He took a stab at her name. "Thloy-are-gan? Dare I ask how to spell that?"

I told him, and his brows shot up. "Are you sure?"

I laughed and got to my feet. "It's Welsh. It means moonlight."

"Yes," Ioan said as he appeared with an antipasto tray. "We're quite certain Liv picked it to be difficult. The double *L* is what's known as a voiceless lateral fricative sound. It's nearly impossible for non-native Welsh speakers to manage correctly. Liv does a fine job of it, though."

"Showing off, is she?" Todd said with a smile.

I stuck out my tongue and gave Lloergan one last pet before taking the wine into the main room. Ioan had the fire going low, taking the spring dampness from the air, and Lloergan lumbered over to lie in front of it.

I motioned Todd to one of the sofas as I opened the wine, and Trahaearn brought in the promised cheese tray.

"So," Ioan said as he settled into an armchair, Brenin beside him. "You have a problem."

I nodded. "We need to know where you bury the bodies."

He gave a short laugh. Then he saw I was serious.

"All right," he said. "That wasn't merely an idiom. You mean the actual corpses of our prey. If there's been a cache of corpses uncovered, I can assure you it's not us. We don't use mass graves, and we don't take enough souls to fill one."

"I'm asking about one body in particular." I glanced at Todd. "Greg Kirkman."

Ioan's surprise lasted only a blink. Then he nodded, relaxing into the chair and turning to Todd. "You were just released from prison, and that is the one thing that could send you back. You're understandably concerned. Let me assure you that his body is well hidden. Even if it was found, the tissue—and any damage to it— would long be gone. Mr. Kirkman has returned to the soil, where he's done far more good in death than he ever did in life."

Ioan leaned forward. "If you have any concern about the righteousness of what you did, Todd, any at *all*, I would gladly set your mind at rest with more details of his crimes. Not the intimate details, of course, but the number of victims, their absolute innocence and his absolute guilt."

"I know he was guilty," Todd said. "He confessed to me, quite happily."

That was what ultimately set Todd off. Kirkman's confession—not the guilt-stricken breakdown of a remorseful man, but the gloating boast of one who lost not a minute of sleep over his crimes.

Ioan continued. "I realize, too, that in the human world, people dislike the death penalty. The permanence of it. The possibility of error. Your own case is a perfect argument against it. Yet we know our targets are guilty. You can ask Liv about that. She's had experience—a case where it seemed we were mistaken. We were not. Even if a man confesses, he still may not have done the crime. But Greg Kirkman did, and there was little chance he'd have served a day in prison. What you did was justice."

"No," Todd said carefully. "What I did was vengeance. A rage-fueled vengeance that was not mine to take. I didn't kill him because it was right or just. In that moment, I wanted him to suffer, as his victims had."

Ioan's expression said he didn't see what difference that made. Todd still killed Kirkman for his crimes. I understood, though. I'd been Todd in his memories. I'd felt that rage, and then felt the shame and horror of what he'd done.

"We aren't asking about Kirkman as a hypothetical," I said. "A body was just found near where Dad...did it."

Ioan relaxed back in his seat again and picked up his wineglass. "Then I understand your concern, but I can assure you, there's no need for it. Greg Kirkman is not there. We wouldn't dispose of his body near where he'd been killed. In the event he was found, we wouldn't want the scene nearby. He's over a mile away."

"Not off Willow Creek Road?"

"No. He's across the highway in a separate area of forest. We rarely transport the body far. We don't want to be pulled over with a body in the trunk. But we put distance between Kirkman and the scene of his death. If a body was found off Willow Creek Road, it's not him."

Ioan's lips pursed. "Could it be his last victim? I know she was there, where you found Kirkman, Todd. We had, unfortunately, no way of leading the authorities to her body without putting you at risk. We'd prefer to give some resolution to the family. In this case, with the…state of her body, and the violence of her death, they'd have had no comfort even if we could have done it. If they've found her body now, though, that damage will be gone, and her family may welcome the closure."

"The police claim it's a man," I said. "Dead about twenty years, apparently just enough remaining tissue to suggest he was the victim of a violent attack."

"Still could be her," Trahaearn said. "I've studied forensics. That's my role in the Pack. I keep current on crime scene analysis, so we don't make any mistakes in our disposal. An unembalmed corpse, buried in soil, will decompose completely within about ten years. Climate conditions can speed up or inhibit that process. However, we didn't bury the girl. As I recall, she'd been left under a fallen tree, sheltered, so Kirkman could…return to her. That may have protected her from complete decay, but I can't imagine there would be enough flesh to make a positive sex identification. Clothing would help, but it'd be in a state of serious decay, too. The police may have jumped to an incorrect default conclusion. A twenty-year-old corpse, showing signs of violence, found off Willow Creek Road? I'd lay bets it's her. That's a mild concern because of her link to Kirkman. It's not as bad as finding him, though."

No, it wasn't nearly as bad as finding him.

EIGHT

GABRIEL

GABRIEL HAD told Olivia he would investigate this by calling his contacts at the state police. He had not lied. At the time he said the words, that had been his intention. Then he hung up, considered the matter, and decided to take a different tack: visiting the scene.

He did, naturally, have a plan for managing the risk. Yet he had to admit he was taking a bigger chance than he should, spurred on not by logic but by emotion. Uncomfortable to admit. Incredibly uncomfortable. But it was a necessary step on a path he needed to travel.

Gabriel had always considered himself a self-aware man. He knew what he was and what he was not. He'd come to realize, though, that what he considered recognizing his shortcomings was actually the act of strengthening them, of accepting them, of using them for excuses. Like when he'd realized he had no aptitude for geometry and promptly dropped the course rather than risk doing poorly in it. Whether he liked geometry had no bearing on his decision. He hated to even remember how many times he'd almost applied that logic to his relationship with Olivia back when they first grew close. He was not good at friendships—and certainly not good at *more* than friendship—and so he should just quit her. Accept his shortcomings and walk away.

Walk away before he got hurt. Before he was disappointed. That's what it really came down to.

Thankfully he'd overcome that before they began dating, and he'd never once since considered walking away. Which led to an entirely new and even less comfortable worry. What if *she* walked away? He'd let his guard down, allowed her into his life, admitted he loved her and wanted to be with her for the rest of that life. The promise ring had been her way of calming his fears, telling him she felt the same.

Yet it was one aspect of that old worry that drove him out of his office today, set him on the road to visit the scene of the body recovery.

The problem was that Gabriel's bòcan blood meant he understood the concept of reciprocity very well. In the past couple of years, it'd begun to manifest in a new and distressing way. Gabriel had not lived an ethical life by any stretch of the imagination. Even as a lawyer, he used blackmail and extortion. He broke into offices and private residences. He pickpocketed phones from police officers and prosecution lawyers and aides. He stole case files. He bribed clerks for access to information he should not have. He had standards, though. He would never plant evidence or bribe a judge or tamper with a jury or blackmail a witness into lying on the stand. That was cheating.

Gabriel did not feel that what he did—in the pursuit of his clients' interests—was wrong. Yet he certainly understood he was committing criminal acts that could cost him his livelihood, could even cost him his freedom. It was a calculated risk.

Now, though, as his life deepened, with Olivia and all that she brought into his world, he had begun to suffer a dread of consequences from the universe itself. It was a concept people like his aunt knew well. Karma. Superstition. Fate. The sense that some universal force measured good deeds against bad. So far, Gabriel had been lucky— inordinately lucky. He'd achieved not only financial and professional success, but now also personal fulfillment. He was happy. Not satisfied. Not content. Happy. The question was: did he deserve it?

No. He was quite certain he did not.

On a rational level, he didn't care. He repaid his good fortune by treating Olivia as she deserved to be treated. He'd also learned to extend that care and respect and consideration more fully to others who deserved it, like Rose, Ricky and Lydia. And together with Olivia, he did good in the fae world, expecting little in return.

Yet beneath his rational side lurked a fretful sort of worry, surfacing only when something sparked it. That call from Olivia had sparked it.

Gabriel had freed Todd from prison. He'd given Olivia the thing she wanted most. Her father free. Her father back in her life.

What if that was too much? What if the universe had said, "Enough"?

Gabriel had freed many guilty clients. It was the job of the legal system to convict them and *his* job to give them the best possible defense. Would it not be ironic if the one person he knew to be innocent went back to prison? Karmic revenge. He'd helped countless criminals avoid charges, and he didn't give a damn about one of them. So when he actually did care, when his client was actually innocent of the charges, was this when he'd lose?

That's what Gabriel had been afraid of, all through the trial. When he'd won his case, he was more relieved than he would ever admit. But now, his bòcan blood whispered, what if the universe wished to correct the imbalance? Was it not greater punishment to send Todd back to prison *after* Gabriel got him out?

It would certainly be worse for Olivia. To see the realization of a dream, only to have it whisked away.

Gabriel had watched clients dissolve into oozing puddles of anxiety. He'd seen them twist into knots of worry. He defended clients guilty of murder and facing life in prison. Men who'd callously and cruelly taken a life, perhaps even boasted about it, only to break down in tears at the prospect of what Gabriel would, privately, call quid pro quo. Take a life, and you risk giving up yours in return. Yet even when Gabriel himself had faced that same sentence for a crime he did not commit, he'd never collapsed. Not outwardly. Not even inwardly. However worried he'd been, he'd tackled the problem with calm resolution.

And so, the fact that this irrational fear of universal karma sent him flying down the highway toward Cainsville did not mean that he was in any danger of curling up in the fetal position, whimpering. Only a vague anxiety floated in his gut, no more noticeable than a cup of strong coffee, drunk too late at night.

He told himself that the universe was not going to punish him. Such things did not happen. There was no karmic scale floating in the ether, no deity weighing his heart against a feather. There was simply a corpse in a forest, uncomfortably close to where Todd had executed Gregory Kirkman. It was an unfortunate coincidence, nothing more. This dead man could not be Kirkman.

Olivia was asking Ioan where they'd disposed of Kirkman. Gabriel already knew the answer to that—not precisely where Kirkman lay, but in general terms, which was "not where he'd been killed." The Cŵn Annwn weren't fools. They wouldn't leave a corpse near a crime scene, especially in the forest where once you moved the body, you lost the scene itself and all forensic evidence that went with it.

Fae could be careless. Flighty, capricious and careless. The Cŵn Annwn were none of that. Olivia often said that she suspected Gabriel of having Cŵn Annwn blood. Like them, he was meticulous in his work, careful and considered. That did not mean Olivia was right. Such traits could come from anywhere. The upshot of this situation was that Gabriel knew this body did not belong to Greg Kirkman. He simply needed to see it for himself, get that answer as quickly as possible and relay it to Olivia and Todd, so they could all stop worrying.

Olivia said Willow Creek Road. It branched off the secondary highway that led to Cainsville. The road was gravel, and he could imagine Olivia wincing with every stone that hit the undercarriage. That lifted his mood, and he relaxed. When he finally spotted the cars, one still had its lights flashing, which would make his story more plausible.

Two state police cars. Dr. Webster's little convertible. One additional unmarked car—detectives, most likely. Another unmarked SUV that he knew would belong to the crime scene techs. A lone officer stood by the cars, doing something on his cell phone.

Gabriel pulled over well behind the last vehicle. The officer's head snapped up at the sound of gravel crunching under the Jaguar's tires. When Gabriel got out, the young man strode over.

"This is a crime scene. If you're with the media, I need to ask you to leave."

Gabriel lifted one brow and looked from his vehicle to the officer, that brow rising again, suggesting that such a car could hardly be purchased on a journalist's salary.

"My name is Gabriel Walsh," he said.

Potential recognition flashed over the officer's face, only to disappear, as if he'd heard the name but couldn't place it.

"I live in Cainsville," Gabriel said, gesturing in the direction of the town. "I was passing when I saw the flashing lights."

The officer didn't pause to consider the possibility of seeing those lights from two miles away. He just said, "All right, sir. I understand that as a local homeowner you are concerned, but I can assure you, we have this under control. Now, I'll need to ask you to leave—"

"Yes, I am a local homeowner, but I am also the attorney of the *land*owner whose property you have apparently discovered a crime on. Have you contacted her?"

The man stopped. Blinked. "Lawyer? Gabriel... You're..."

"Yes, I said that. Now, the landowner. Has she been contacted?"

The officer kept blinking, clearly in shock at meeting the famous Gabriel Walsh and fighting the urge to shake Gabriel's hand and commend him on his fine work...

Gabriel smiled inwardly at that. No, "famous" wasn't quite the word he'd use. More like infamous. And officers of the law *never* lauded his contributions to their field. It was terribly disappointing.

"Walsh." The young man straightened, and his voice dropped two octaves. "I need you out of here. If you've come ambulance chasing—"

"Do you see an ambulance? I have no need to chase clients in any manner. I am here representing one, and so I'll return to the question I have now asked twice. Have you contacted the landowner?"

The young man looked at the forest.

"Yes, that is private property," Gabriel said. "You will note the lack of signs indicating this is a public recreation area."

"There aren't *any* signs. If it was private property—"

"You grew up in Chicago, didn't you?"

"Yes, but—"

"You are a member of the state police. Judging by your youth, you have not been one long. You may even still live in the city."

With your parents, Gabriel thought, though he did not add it. "But it behooves you to acquire a better understanding of your rural working environment. Most land here is privately owned, even if it is not currently in use. Landowners rarely post signs. People are free to walk through these woods. You'll find paths for that purpose. But it is owned by a family in Cainsville, who has owned most of this land for nearly two centuries. I represent the current matriarch of that family, Grace Clark."

"No one told me it was private land."

"Understandably. A crime has been committed, as you said, and I would not want the police to stand on this road trying to find the landowner while a victim suffers or a suspect escapes."

The officer snorted. "Your job is *letting* them escape."

"My job is defending them, which I cannot do if they aren't arrested. Now, the law, rightfully, says that you may enter this property in pursuit of justice. I am not disputing that. However, the law also says that my client has the right to know what is happening on her land."

Not entirely true, but if this young man had a law degree, he wouldn't be guarding a crime scene.

"Would you like to speak to my client?" Gabriel asked. "I can call her. I can even bring her out here. However, I'll warn you she's elderly, and she will not appreciate being forced to come out when she has given permission for me, as her representative—"

The officer didn't let Gabriel finish. He was already on his radio, telling another officer that he had the landowner's legal representative here. He did not, Gabriel noted, say *who* that representative was. That wasn't an oversight, Gabriel suspected. The young officer had had enough of Gabriel and wished to foist him onto someone else, quickly.

Gabriel didn't know the young woman who came out. Truly, sometimes he felt so much older than his thirty years, faced with the continual influx of young officers, recognizing none, and knowing that by the time he did, they'd have moved on. Which was, of course, a fine excuse for never bothering to ask names in the first place.

The young woman treated him with the same indifference. He was a lawyer, and that's all she needed to know. She waved for him to follow her, and he did.

The woods did indeed belong to Grace. They'd originally belonged to Ida, but on her death, they'd passed to her "cousin." Capricious didn't describe all fae, and those who settled Cainsville had chosen their refuge with all the care he expected the Cŵn Annwn had used in finding a final resting place for Gregory Kirkman. At the time, Cainsville would have seemed an impossibly long distance from Chicago, but they'd had the foresight to imagine a future when that might change. These days, Cainsville should have been a bedroom community for the big city. It was not. The land surrounding the town—a river on one side, swampy land on others—forbade expansion. When the highway was built, they'd made sure no exit would lead directly to the town, instead forcing drivers to backtrack along the secondary highway. They'd also bought land, thousands of acres, purchased when it'd sold for laughably little. Over the years, Ida had allowed Cainsville families to purchase rural building lots, but those holdings were small, and the remainder had been hers.

This forest represented the border of Ida's—now Grace's— holdings. Beyond it lay a village and roads dotted with homes belonging to people with no connection to Cainsville. Kirkman himself had owned one of those houses, which was why he had used this forest to hide at least one victim.

As they approached, Gabriel could hear voices, and he slowed to listen. They weren't saying anything useful, though. Quite the contrary. They were discussing what they'd done on the weekend.

A couple of detectives were watching Dr. Webster, who bent over something out of his view, presumably the body. It was the detectives chatting. Dr. Webster was busy, as were the crime scene techs, one taking pictures while another worked deeper in the forest.

The officer leading Gabriel said, "The lawyer."

One of the detectives turned. When she saw Gabriel, she let out a sharp laugh. "The lawyer indeed. You don't know who that is, Tina?"

The young woman's face screwed up as she looked at Gabriel. "He's not a lawyer?"

"Oh, hell, yeah," Detective Parsons said. "He's definitely a lawyer. May I present Gabriel Walsh, scourge of the Chicago PD."

"Scourge?" Gabriel said. "That's rather harsh, don't you think?"

"Not at all."

"Also, one might say, incorrect," Gabriel said. "If I am the scourge of anyone, it would be the state attorney's office. It's their cases I overturn. My actions have no effect on the clearance rates of the detectives involved, which is really all that matters to the police."

"Ouch. And touché."

There was no rancor in Detective Parsons's voice. Gabriel had worked with her before, and she was one of the rare officers who seemed to understand the necessity of his job. It helped that her brother had, according to Gabriel's research, spent two years incarcerated in the eighties for a crime he did not commit. A defense lawyer set him free.

Parsons was, in fact, the "contact" Gabriel would have called on this case. He had two classes of police contacts. One, he bought. They gave him information in return for "monetary consideration for their time and effort." The second group were the cultivated contacts, the ones he traded with on a professional—and completely legal—basis. He could ask Detective Parsons for information, and if she could share it, she would. In return, if she had legal questions—points of law she needed clarified for a case—she called him.

When she said his name, the other detective snorted and walked off with the young officer.

Dr. Webster had also heard Gabriel's name, and her head had popped up. Gabriel wouldn't say she smiled, but her grim expression relaxed, and she nodded, friendly enough. She was indeed crouched beside a body, blocking it.

"Do you really represent the landowner, or did you just say that to get back here?" Parsons asked.

"I am one of the town's legal representatives," Gabriel said. "As Dr. Webster can attest."

Parsons looked around pointedly. "The nearest town is two miles away, counselor."

"No, that is a village. I am referring to Cainsville. This land is held in trust by the town and owned by Grace Clark."

Dr. Webster looked up. "The town owns this far out?" She whistled and shook her head. Then she looked up at the detective. "Not that I'm questioning. Trust me, if Gabriel says they do, then they do. That's what you get when your family has been here forever, and they had the forethought not to sell at the first good offer. I can't even imagine what it's all worth now."

"Enough for the town to employ me in addition to their civil legal team."

Dr. Webster chuckled. "True." She sat back on her haunches. "You can let Grace know about this." She waved at the body.

Gabriel walked around it, examining from all angles. It was, as Olivia suggested, a very old corpse. She'd mentioned signs of trauma. Those might exist, but if they did, they wouldn't be evident without a forensic exam. This was not the decayed body he'd expected. It was a skeleton. The skeleton of a person not much more than five feet tall, with long dark hair. A skeleton wearing a dress.

"A woman," he said.

This time, it was both the doctor and the detective who chuckled.

"Very astute, Gabriel," Dr. Webster said. "Though, perhaps I shouldn't laugh. The body's size and the hair—and even the dress—don't confirm gender. From the pubic bone, though, I can say with near certainty that we're looking at a young woman, likely pubescent."

"A teenager," Gabriel murmured.

This made sense. Perfect sense, and relief fluttered through him. They were in the forest behind where Kirkman had lived. The forest where Todd had seen the body of Kirkman's last victim hidden under a tree fall. The body of a teenage girl.

The officer in the diner had probably heard that a twenty-year-old corpse had been uncovered and leapt to the dual false conclusion it'd been buried and male.

"Signs of trauma?" Gabriel asked.

Dr. Webster nodded. "Cut marks on the bones. Lots of them. Some are scavenging, but there's nothing bigger than a fox out here. I suspect blade marks."

"Young woman murdered and dumped in a forest."

"Were there any serial killers active in the area during that time period?" Dr. Webster asked.

Parsons looked at Gabriel, and her mouth opened. Then she stopped.

"Yes, Detective?" Gabriel said.

"You know who I was going to suggest, Walsh. I stopped because I was about to make a joke, and then I remembered that

Todd Larsen's also your girlfriend's father, and you would not appreciate my humor. Not that you would at the best of times, but it would be disrespectful now, under the circumstances."

"I realize the time period fits the crimes for which my clients were accused. However, this"—he pointed to the body—"does not."

Parsons nodded. "The Valentine Killer targeted couples in their twenties. They were strangled, not stabbed. I never thought Todd was guilty anyway. I met him—him and Pamela—during the initial investigation."

Gabriel glanced at her.

"No, I never mentioned that, Walsh. I knew better. I was just a rookie then anyway. I doubt my name is in the files. If I told you I thought Todd was innocent, you'd have hauled me onto the stand as a damned character witness. No thank you. Especially since Pamela was your original client. I didn't get the same vibe from her. Todd was a sweetheart. Easy on the eyes, too, I'll admit, but just a nice guy. He lacked the edge. She had it. Not that I think she did it. I'm just saying I could imagine her killing someone, but not Todd. So I'm glad he's free. I'll even wish you good luck getting Pamela out, for your girlfriend's sake." Parsons paused. "Does she still go by Olivia?"

Gabriel and Dr. Webster both nodded.

"I knew her as Eden," Parsons said. "Todd talked about her. A doting daddy, that one. I always wondered what became of her. I remember hoping she had a good life wherever she was."

"She did."

"And yet she ended up with you. Poor kid. Did she dig past the rough exterior and find your deeply hidden heart of gold?"

"No, she's decided I'm an acceptable partner despite my lack of it."

Parsons grinned. "I know her adoptive mother was a philanthropist. A tireless champion of lost causes. That must help."

"It does."

As Parsons and Dr. Webster laughed, Gabriel looked at the young woman's corpse. No, the universe did *not* balance good deeds with bad. This girl had done nothing to deserve death, and certainly not the horrific one she'd endured. As for Gabriel's own misdeeds, the universe apparently wasn't punishing him for them just yet.

He opened his mouth to exchange a few final words with the women because both deserved his civility. His mind, however, was already leaping twenty minutes ahead when he could call and tell Olivia all was well.

I understood your distress. I wanted answers for you, faster than I could get them with a phone call. There is no need to worry. Your father is fine and—

"Okay, doc," the young female officer said, coming through the forest. "They've finished digging up the second body. You can take a look at him now."

NINE

OLIVIA

BEFORE I left Ioan's, I'd texted Gabriel to ask whether he could grab dinner on his way home. Turned out he was already home and cooking, which was kind of awesome. There's that old saying that the way to a man's heart is through his stomach, and I could understand at least part of that. It wasn't the food that made me swoon. It was having someone cook for me.

My adoptive parents didn't cook. We *had* a cook. Yes, we were that kind of wealthy. I grew up with a succession of lovely ladies making me amazing meals, and I cannot complain about that. I could have learned from them, but in that world, cooking was something other people did, and I appreciated the hell out of them for it.

Then the revelation of my birth parents came, and I walked away from that life, determined to make it on my own. Relishing the challenge, to be honest. I was like the suburban kid who thinks milking cows looks cool. I had no idea how tough life was without money. I learned, though. Got an apartment at Grace's. Worked in the diner. Learned to cook. Eventually even learned to cook things that were edible.

I'd never had someone who cared about me and made me food. Gabriel does, and I love doing the same for him. There's a meaning in it, beyond simply "Well, we have to eat, and I'm less busy/tired, so I'll do it." Maybe it was just because I'd never had that before, but it felt special to me.

Coming home to a ready meal wasn't nearly as common, considering we worked together. The very thought had me cranking up the tunes, hitting the gas, and singing along as I drove home, to the great amusement of my father. That wasn't the wine. I'd had less than a glass—my recklessness didn't extend to drinking and driving. From what Ioan said, we had nothing to worry about. Kirkman's body wasn't in those woods. Whoever they'd found had died in an unconnected event.

I told Gabriel my news as soon as I got inside. He was busy with his stir-fry, and he didn't turn from the stove when I broke the news. He just grunted and kept stirring. I smiled and shook my head at that. God forbid he seem surprised, let alone relieved.

I chattered through the meal, still riding my high. Afterward, I shooed Gabriel away, and Todd and I cleared the dishes.

"I'm going to go for a walk," Todd said as we finished up.

"Sure, we can…" I caught his expression. "Ah, *you* want to go for one."

"I thought I'd give you two some alone time," he said, "without me retreating to my room like a sullen teenager. It's a nice night, and I'd like to prowl about a bit. Explore the town." He paused. "No one will have a problem with that, will they?"

I shook my head. "You might be cornered for small talk, but you're safe."

He made a face.

"I mean you're safe from anything like what happened at the restaurant. Only about five percent of Cainsville are full-blooded fae, but the elders work charms here. Wards against trouble and… well, other things. Compulsion magic that keeps people drinking the Kool-Aid. Keeps them from questioning. Keeps them accepting the town's quirks. If the elders say you're welcome here, then you're welcome."

"I'll need to get used to *not* being welcome," he said. "But I'll take this for now."

After he left, I refilled my wine and headed to the dining room where Gabriel worked. As I passed through the hall, I spotted Todd's cell phone by the front door. I jogged over and threw open the door, but he was already down the road. Calling him back really would make him feel like a teenager, Mom freaking out at him leaving without his phone.

I headed into the dining room to find Gabriel standing at the window, staring out. At first, I thought he was watching Todd go. Then I realized Todd had walked the other way, and Gabriel's laptop still sat on the table, unopened.

When I walked behind him and put my hands around his waist, he gave a start. I backed up and said, "Hey," as he turned. It took a moment for him to nod, murmuring something similar. He didn't meet my gaze, his eyes empty, his mind elsewhere. He snapped out of it in a blink, leaning to kiss my cheek and then walking to his laptop.

"I spoke to our new client today," he said. "It was certainly interesting."

That was my opening. Now, I'd say, "Interesting how?" in anticipation of a good story. Yesterday, he'd told me about this new client

as a distraction. Today, he did the same…to distract me from noticing his distant gaze and closed laptop. I could be a shitty girlfriend,
too wrapped up in my own drama to notice anything wrong with
him. He'd been quiet during dinner, engaged but adding little, letting me prattle on because it kept me from noticing his own mood.

When I didn't ask, "Interesting how?" a look passed over his
face. One so subtle and fleeting only I would notice. Panic. He'd
dangled the bait, and I hadn't jumped for it.

He continued to the table, his chin down, gaze on his laptop as
he sat and popped it open.

"He's blaming the dog now," Gabriel said. "Yes, apparently, yesterday, when he tried to blame his ex-wife, my reaction suggested he
could do better. So now, it's the dog."

"Gabriel?"

His fingers tensed over the keyboard. Then he quickly tapped
keys, opening applications with a casual, "Hmm?"

"You left your wine in the kitchen. Would you like it?"

His shoulders relaxed. "Yes, please. Thank you."

"I'll bring it into the living room. We can talk there."

A pause, fingers poised over the keys again. His mouth opened,
and I knew he sensed a trap. He was about to say, no, he really had
so much to do, and he'd tell me his story while he worked.

"Todd's gone for a walk," I said. "We have an empty house
and"—I lifted my glass—"excellent wine, bought for me by my
awesome boyfriend. Let's relax for a few minutes. I'd love to hear the
rest of that story."

The tension eased again, and he nodded and rose. I retrieved his
wine and found him in the parlor, lighting the fireplace.

"There's a chill," he said.

Yes, there is. But it's not the weather.

I let him finish. Then he settled beside me on the sofa, and I set my wineglass down and turned, pulling my feet up, my back resting against him. He relaxed more at that. I was curled up with him, not looking at him, relaxed and clearly not the least bit suspicious.

"So what's wrong?" I said.

I swore I heard the mental "Shit!" as he stiffened. I inched down the sofa, flopped my head onto his lap and gazed up at him.

"No, I wasn't fooled. Yes, I trapped you here before I called you on it. Nasty trick. I learned from the best."

He stayed tense. Then he relaxed with a snort, and his hand went to my hair, stroking it off my face. A careful touch, as if even after a year together, he was ready for me to object.

"I love you," I said.

His chin dipped, eyelids dropping just a fraction. Closing the blinds so I wouldn't see past them. He didn't answer, and that, along with those shuttered eyes, told me everything I needed to know. My gut clenched, a voice inside screaming something was wrong, really wrong, something he didn't want to tell me because I'd been in a good mood, and he wanted to leave me there.

This was serious.

This was about me.

"Gabriel?" I said, struggling to keep my expression neutral.

Not freaking out. Nope, not at all.

"I love you," he said. He didn't add the "too." He said it as if I hadn't. His fingers brushed my cheek, moving aside hair no longer coiled there.

"I love you, too," I said. I forced a smile. "And if you're trying to distract me from my question, you know that's not going to—"

"I would like to discuss Gregory Kirkman," he said, as if he hadn't realized I was speaking, lost in his own thoughts.

"Okay," I said. "But Ioan assured me—"

"I would like to discuss the concern this raises," he said. "Your father *has* done something that could send him back to prison. He is innocent of the crimes for which he was convicted, but this other issue lingers, and I believe we should address that."

"I agree." I sat and twisted to face him. "I *would* like to discuss that. However well the Cŵn Annwn hid Kirkman, this scare reminds us that the possibility exists."

"I would handle it."

"I'm not asking for—"

"That's what I wanted to say. That I am prepared for the possibility, and I would handle it. First, let me point out a discovered body would by no means implicate your father. He knew Kirkman from working with him on a job. They were not friends. Outside of that job, he had no contact with the man prior to the incident. Todd told no one he was going to that forest. Told no one what he suspected. He did not leave a trail of any kind, and forensic evidence would be long gone. In short, I cannot imagine that he would even be questioned in Kirkman's death, should the man's body be found."

"I know."

Gabriel exhaled, as if he'd been holding his breath. "Good. Now, to take it farther and cover all eventualities, let's imagine he is not only questioned but arrested and put on trial. I would be there. I would defend him. I would…I would fix this."

At that last hesitation, his shoulders squared, as if reassuring not only me but himself. *Yes, I have this. Yes, I could do this. Never fear. I will fix it for you, Olivia.*

"I don't need you to do that," I said. "But thank you. You did everything in your power to get my father out. If anything—" I cleared my throat, covering the hitch in my voice. "If anything happened now, I know you'd do your best, and I'd know that nothing—nothing—is guaranteed. Todd did what he did. We understand why. A court would not. I accept that. So does he."

Gabriel nodded, and I thought I'd said exactly the right thing, but his gaze went distant again, and his nod continued a little too long.

"Gabriel? If you're worrying, then I appreciate that, too, but you're right. They're not going to find Kirkman and even if they did—"

"They have."

He blurted the words and then looked horrified. He didn't take them back, though. Didn't apologize or stammer out an explanation. This was Gabriel. He realized his mistake, took two seconds to regroup, and followed through.

"The body is almost certainly Gregory Kirkman's. He had identification. His social security card."

"Then someone planted it on another body. Or there's been a mistake. Ioan buried Kirkman miles away from that spot."

"Yes. I know, and I'm not questioning that. But I went to the site. I know the detective in charge, and I was there with the bodies."

"Bodies? Plural?"

"They also found what appears to be the skeletal remains of Kirkman's last victim, only a few yards from where he was buried."

"But that's—that's not what happened. That isn't possible." I got to my feet and began to pace. "The Cŵn Annwn buried Kirkman miles away. They wouldn't have left him with his ID. And a social security card? Not a driver's license or health insurance or credit card?"

Gabriel said nothing. He was waiting for me to work it through, to come to the obvious conclusion, no matter how far-fetched.

When you have eliminated the impossible, whatever remains, however improbable, must be the truth.

I turned to Gabriel. "How was he found?"

I knew the answer to this. Once you put everything else together, there was only one rational explanation. I still asked, and he said exactly what I expected.

"The police received an anonymous tip."

"More than a tip, right? They got instructions for where to dig."

"Yes, the tip was very specific. The ground had been disturbed. The police believe the call may have come from the repentant killer. Or perhaps a repentant accomplice—someone who knew the body was there, went looking, and called once they'd found him."

"Meaning someone moved his body from where the Cŵn Annwn left it. Disturbing the soil, allegedly to confirm Kirkman was there, would cover up the relocation of the body, at least to the casual eye. The ID card was planted. Someone had it—or found it—and left it with the body."

"Yes, I believe so."

"So my father is released from prison, and a day later, his one actual victim is unearthed and reported to the police. Someone's setting Todd up. He'll be connected to Kirkman's murder and arrested and—"

"Not necessarily," Gabriel said. "This isn't a human looking for revenge. It must be fae, which means it isn't about justice. It never is with them."

"It's manipulation. It's the threat of putting him back in prison. Leverage. We need to get ahead of it."

"We *are* ahead of it," Gabriel said. "Now we need to stay there."

TEN

OLIVIA

GABRIEL AND I talked for the next hour. My panic passed; I'd moved back to the sofa, lying on his lap as we worked through it. He was right. No human knew where to find that body or how it connected to my father. A fae moved it, and now they'd hold that threat over us in return for a favor. Of course.

We were Matilda and Gwynn, and we were still navigating that. We needed to strike a balance between using it to our advantage and not being taken advantage of. We weren't just humans—we were young humans. To the fae, that was like having a child crowned queen without any vice-regent to guide her. The perfect pawn to exploit.

I could bitch to the elders about this—*See what a shitty position I'm in, for your sake*—but in truth, Gabriel and I reveled in it. We'd get what we could out of the arrangement. Making sure the balance stayed in our favor only added challenge.

Earlier, Gabriel had assured me that if my father was arrested, he'd "fix" it, but *this* was where it could be fixed. Before any arrest.

We knew what was happening. We were prepared for our fae opponent's next move. It would be an anonymous e-mail or a newspaper left on our step, someone calling attention to the discovery of Kirkman's body. The fae involved would sit back and let us stew and work ourselves into a frenzy. Then they'd make contact with the offer. *Oh, hey, about that body—I know your dad did it, Matilda, but I'll keep that to myself, in return for...*

In return for refuge in Cainsville.

In return for an audience with the Cŵn Annwn.

In return for one million dollars.

The last was unlikely—fae traded in favors and favor—but it could happen. It didn't matter. We knew what was coming and only had to sit tight and wait.

I was rising to refill my wineglass when I noticed the parlor window darkening as night fell. I checked my watch and scrambled up. "Todd went for a walk after dinner. Two hours ago."

"I thought I heard him in the kitchen. He may have come back and heard us talking."

That made sense, and someone *was* in the kitchen—TC, chowing down. Otherwise, the lower floor was shrouded in darkness, lights out. I flicked them on as I walked.

"Dad?" I called.

I jogged up to his bedroom. The door creaked open when I knocked. Empty. I clambered back down the stairs as the patio door whooshed.

I exhaled in relief and strode into the kitchen only to find Gabriel locking the sliding door.

"I thought he might be out there," Gabriel said. "But I'm sure it's fine. The elders probably stopped him to talk. I'll give him a call, though."

He was already on his phone. Before I could say anything, Todd's phone in the front hall rang.

"He left it behind," I said. "I saw it, but I didn't want to make a big deal. Damn it. I should have gone after him."

Gabriel squeezed my elbow as he passed. "If he's been waylaid, it's by a curious resident. No one will harm him here, Olivia."

He said this as he continued to the front door, where he picked up his loafers. Reassuring me that all was fine…while getting his shoes, knowing I would not be content to sit and drink my wine and trust my father was okay.

"Thank you," I said.

His glance asked, *For what?* and I just smiled as he tugged on a loafer. Then I pulled on my sneakers and followed him out.

GABRIEL and I separated. This was, as he said, Cainsville. No need for us to stick side by side. No need for me to bring my gun along, either. In preparation for Todd's arrival, Veronica had put extra wards on the town, which she said guaranteed no fae would slip in undetected. The wards required too much energy to run all the time, but they were on this week. Trespassing fae would be spotted by the owls or the gargoyles. Yes, gargoyles.

For me, the disappearing gargoyles had been Cainsville's greatest mystery. The elders—Ida in particular—had held that answer out to me as a carrot. As soon as I agreed to be their Matilda, I'd discovered the truth about the gargoyles. When I did, it was like solving the mystery of Santa Claus, truly one of the biggest disappointments in my life.

As a child, I drove my parents crazy asking how Santa delivered to every child in one night. My dad said that when I was older, he'd tell me, and I'd lived for that day when I expected he'd reveal some combination of science and magic that answered all my questions. Then I learned the truth. No magic. Not even science. Just parents creating stories for their children.

The gargoyles *were* magic and science combined. I'd give them that much. They were stone guardians that functioned as a magical alert system. The eyes of the elders, like the owls. Unlike the owls, they were stationary because, well, they were stone. They appeared and disappeared because the magic cast on them cost energy the fae couldn't afford. Rather like powering a high-tech security system in an old house with bad wiring. Having me live in Cainsville would repair that wiring, but that took time.

If Todd encountered a problem, it would come from a resident. Harassment, rather than actual danger.

It turned out such fears were not unfounded. I was walking along a side street when I spotted Todd in one of the town's many walkways, this one cutting behind the school. And he was indeed being harassed. By someone who *didn't* belong in Cainsville. It was a blond guy less than half Todd's age. A couple of inches taller than my father. Broad shoulders under a snug T-shirt. Muscular biceps, one bearing a tattoo. He wore heavy boots and had a leather jacket slung over one arm, and he pushed a Harley along as he bothered my poor father.

When I saw him, I picked up my pace, ready to tell him to leave Todd alone. I also grinned. Grinned as any lingering anxiety floated away.

Ricky was home, and seeing him felt the same as it always had when he'd been away. My steps lightened. My heart lightened, too, as a burst of pure joy sparked through me.

When Ricky and I had been together, that initial joy at his return had, of course, given way to other thoughts of what his return portended. My boyfriend's back, and I'm gonna get laid. Yet my first reaction had always been simple happiness at seeing him, at the return, not of my lover, but of my friend. Now, when Ricky comes home, I only get the first response.

I'd forgotten Ricky was returning today. He'd texted while I'd been talking to Gabriel, and I'd meant to look at it once we were done, but then I'd forgotten in my worry over Todd. Ricky must have been telling me he'd landed and was heading over. He'd spotted Todd and stopped to walk with him.

As I veered into the passageway, I grinned to myself and then backed out. They were strolling through an empty green-space, lined with trees, shadows stretching. Sneaking up on them would be incredibly immature. Also, incredibly fun.

Staying behind a manicured spruce, I surveyed the playing field. If I backed out, I could loop along another way, jump out and give them a start. Yep, terribly immature. Which never stopped me.

I took one last look around, making sure they wouldn't see me when I came down the other passage. No, I'd be fine. Just back out and run—

A shape moved in the greenery. I went still, narrowing my eyes. I saw nothing there. Just shrubs and shadows. Ricky's voice drifted to me as he answered a question about the bike. He stopped and pointed something out on it, and Todd crouched for a better look.

The shrubs rippled. I blinked and focused on the spot. Another ripple, and it seemed as if the air itself blurred.

Fae.

Several subtypes had the ability to blend with their surroundings. They couldn't disappear altogether, but they took advantage of natural camouflage and tricked the human eye. If we knew they were there, though, we'd see the telltale haze, like the blurring I saw right now.

I rolled my shoulders and pushed back sparks of alarm. We were in Cainsville. Of course, there were fae. One had been taking this passageway, maybe without a glamour, and rather than pull it back on, had blended into the shrubs to let Todd and Ricky pass. Or perhaps the fae had heard them coming and didn't feel like chatting, and had literally faded into the background.

Todd and Ricky started walking again. Todd said something, and Ricky laughed, and I glanced over at the sound. When I looked back to the fae's hiding spot, that haze was gone. I squinted, studying the spot. Then I saw it again…on the move, following Todd and Ricky.

They were ambling along, stopping as Ricky pointed out a half-hidden gargoyle. When they paused, that blur did, too.

I slid along the shadows. Todd walked over to examine the gargoyle, which sat under a bush.

"Technically, they're grotesques," Ricky said as Todd lifted a branch to take a better look. "A gargoyle perches on a roof and diverts water. A grotesque is any gargoyle-like figure that doesn't serve that purpose. You can thank your daughter for that bit of trivia. She's the one who knows her architecture. The locals still call these gargoyles. Even Liv does. She hates to sound pedantic."

Todd chuckled. His tone said he wasn't quite sure what the last word meant, but he got the gist of it in context.

The blur continued toward them. It had picked up speed now that they'd stopped, their backs to it while they discussed the local gargoyles. I crept along, rolling my feet, moving silently on the grass.

I drew near enough to see the figure of a woman, faint, like a hologram. It pulsed in and out of my vision, one second clearly a woman, the next no more than an indistinct smudge. She was less than three feet from my father. Right behind him as they chatted unaware.

She crouched to spring. I lunged to knock her flying and—

And then I was on the ground. Flat on my back, pain slamming through me, as if I'd been hit by a wrecking ball. I sprang up, ready to fight.

Ricky and Todd rushed toward me. I opened my mouth to warn them about the fae, but she was gone. I spun, looking for that telltale blur. I caught a flicker of motion off to my left up by the roof. When I looked, though, it was an owl, gliding to rest on the roof's edge. It peered down at me and hooted.

I spun again, looking around.

Ricky caught my arm. "Liv?"

"Did you see that?" I said.

"See what?"

"There was a fae stalking you two. I saw the shimmer of her, and she was about to attack, so I lunged and…"

I looked at the spot where I'd fallen. As I twisted, pain shot through my side, so hard I winced.

"Are you okay, sweetheart?" Todd asked, taking over for Ricky, supporting me.

"I'm fine. I just…" I winced again and rubbed my side.

Todd led me to a bench and insisted I sit.

"What did you see?" I asked.

"You, flat on your back," Ricky said. "I heard a thud and a thump, and when I turned, you were lying there."

Todd nodded. "That's what I heard. Exactly that. Like someone hit you—hard—and you went down."

Which was what happened. I had to struggle to even remember being hit, it happened so fast. The wrecking ball analogy was a good one. A single rock-hard blow. What kind of fae could do that? I had no idea, but I was sure as hell going to find out.

ELEVEN

OLIVIA

I CALLED Gabriel. I told him we'd found Todd, and Ricky was with him. I was sending them back to the house, and I'd appreciate it if Gabriel met them there. I needed to speak to the elder most likely to explain this situation to me: Veronica.

I headed to her house. Pepper answered the door. Pepper was…I guess you'd call her Veronica's ward. To the non-fae in town, she's an exchange student from Greece. In reality, she was a damaged lamiae—a Greek subtype of fae—whom Veronica took under her wing, giving her shelter and letting the town's energy heal her. When I met Pepper last year, she was the developmental equivalent of a five-year-old, and even holding her glamour in place took more energy than she could afford.

Today, the fae who answered the door looked like a teenage girl. That was the lamiae's only choice for a human glamour. Now, though, when she smiled and when she welcomed me in, she really was that teenager, not the child I'd first met.

"Hey, Liv," she said as she opened the door. "Come on in. Is everything okay?"

"I just had a nasty run-in with a fae," I said. "I was hoping to talk to Veronica about it."

Pepper waved me inside. "Veronica's lying down, but if you're trying to figure out what kind it is, I might be able to help. I'm becoming something of an expert." She picked up a book she must have just set down on the front table. "Patrick's been letting me read through his library. Now that I actually *can* read. Gives me something to do until the elders agree I'm well enough to actually get a job." She gestured me through to the kitchen. "Did you see it in the city? Or in the countryside?"

"In town."

That made her turn sharply. "In Cainsville?"

"That's why I wanted to talk to Veronica. There was a fae stalking my father. A woman. She tried to attack him. I jumped in to stop her and ended up on the ground."

Her eyes rounded. "What? That shouldn't—that can't happen. Veronica has the wards up. All the wards. With your dad coming home, she wasn't taking any chances."

She turned toward the stairs leading up to the second story and presumably the bedrooms.

"I know she's resting," I said, "but I really do need to talk to her."

"Right. Totally. Except…she's not just resting. She's in a…" Pepper fluttered her hands. "I don't know how to describe it. A trance? A coma? She's unconscious, and if I wake her, I'll break the wards, and it'll take hours for her to get them back in place."

"Unconscious?"

"Like…" Another flutter as she searched for words. "Like when you're using a generator, and you can either run ten small appliances or one big one. Veronica needs all her power for these wards. So she's shut down her body. It's a fae thing. Like hibernation, maybe? Sorry, I'm not describing this well. The words still don't always come. I know what I mean, but I can't quite articulate it."

"No, you're making sense. Veronica has diverted all her energy to the wards. Unless it's an emergency, we shouldn't wake her."

"Right. If it's urgent, I'll definitely do that, but what exactly happened?"

I told her.

When I finished, Pepper was nodding, processing. "You saw a fae following your father. It looked like she was going to attack him. No local fae would ever hurt your dad. And the wards are working. They must be, or Veronica would wake up. Is it possible the fae wasn't actually preparing to attack? That she made a sudden move, which you understandably interpreted as an attack?"

"It's possible."

"I know the local fae are curious about your dad. Fae are curious." She smiled. "It's one thing we all have in common, whatever our subtype. Maybe one snuck up for a closer look. She moved toward him, and you went after her, and she reacted on instinct. When she realized who she'd hit, she took off. Is that plausible?"

I considered. It was indeed plausible. When I said so, Pepper said, "I'll still wake Veronica if you'd like."

I shook my head. "No, the more I think about it, the more I think you might be right. In any event, I'm fine, and Todd's safe. I'll talk to Gabriel. If he's concerned, we'll speak to the elders."

ONCE I returned home, I got the best part of my day. Whatever crap we were dealing with, there was nothing quite like curling up in my parlor, working through a problem with Gabriel and Ricky. It reminded me how lucky I was to have them in my life. Not just people to solve problems with, but people who also enjoyed this aspect of our lives. Nothing got our blood pumping like mystery and danger and, yes, trouble. A challenge to be faced and vanquished and an adrenalin rush to enjoy.

Given that my father was the one in danger, that certainly dampened my enthusiasm. I worried what he'd think, seeing us attack this problem with more excitement than might be proper. Yet that night, working through the possibilities and the solutions, he came more alive than I'd ever seen him. More engaged. More relaxed, too, as odd as that sounded. I understood it, though. We were tackling his problem with gusto, treating it—despite some unseemly enthusiasm—with all the gravity it deserved. We took it seriously. We were prepared. We were capable. We had this under control...or, if he believed so, well, a vote of confidence never hurt. I just hoped we lived up to his expectations.

Tomorrow, we expected our fae adversary to make his or her move. News of Kirkman's unearthing would hit the papers, and whoever was behind this would ensure we knew about that ASAP.

Our second avenue of investigation came from the other end of the chain. Who could have known where to find Kirkman's body? It was a very short list. Our adversary had also known where to find the body of his last victim and had moved him there. That information almost certainly came from the Cŵn Annwn, however unwittingly.

Ricky would speak to Ioan about that. He was their Arawn, and he had as much leverage there as Gabriel did here in Cainsville. This was where Gabriel would concentrate his own efforts—he wanted to know who'd attacked me tonight. He'd follow up on that. As for me, well, I got the exciting job of waiting for that message from our adversary—the e-mail or whatever they'd send to say, *Hey, look whose body just turned up!*

TWELVE

RICKY

AS RICKY turned onto Ioan's road, he slowed his bike and rolled his shoulders against a crick in his neck. That's what he got with three hours of sleep spent on Liv's couch.

He could have gone home, of course. He had a proper one now—a farmhouse equidistant from his dad's place, Ioan's and the clubhouse, close enough to each to be convenient, far enough for privacy. The privacy part was important. While no one hovered over him, he felt the weight of their expectations, the weight of their gazes. Ricky was Ioan's Arawn, and his father's heir, and the Saints' future leader. Everyone had a vested interest in his future. Liv might joke that Ricky was the most mature and responsible twenty-two-year-old she'd ever met, but he was still twenty-two, and he needed time and space to himself. Time when he could kick back with a beer and Netflix and not have someone hanging over his shoulder, suggesting more productive uses for the two hours of the day he wasn't working his ass off.

So maybe, after five days working that ass off in Miami, he should have been happy for the excuse to go to his new house and sleep in complete peace and quiet. Except...well, to be honest, the whole happy homeowner thing wasn't working out as well as he'd expected. His house felt...empty. Yep, he was whining about the exact thing he'd claimed he wanted. Without even Lloergan there, he'd been in no rush to get home, even if it would have meant a proper bed.

Spending the evening with Liv and Gabriel certainly hadn't made his empty house any more inviting. Ricky was a pack animal. Maybe it was his Cŵn Annwn side. Maybe it was growing up in a motorcycle club. He liked being surrounded by people. He just didn't like the expectations that came with that these days.

Liv and Gabriel expected nothing except the pleasure of his company, and if anything, they could commiserate with the rest, being in the same position. Well, Liv commiserated. Gabriel allowed Ricky to bitch and didn't check his phone or start answering e-mail, which he'd been known to do when a conversation bored him. He listened, and that told Ricky he sympathized, and Ricky knew he was dealing with the same pressures as Gwynn, even if *Gabriel* would never whine about that...or anything else, damn him.

Ricky rolled slowly along Ioan's road, his helmet off as he listened for a familiar sound. When he heard it, he smiled and waited until he saw a flash of black fur. Then he hit the accelerator. The bike took off in a cloud of dust as Lloergan appeared. She fell in beside the bike, running full out. Ricky veered into Ioan's lane and up the drive. When he stopped, Lloergan jumped up, massive paws on his leg, and he braced the bike to keep it from toppling. Then he rubbed and scratched her head.

"You heard me even farther away this time," he said. "Your ears are getting better. You kept up, too. Forty miles an hour."

He whistled and shook his head, and Lloergan whined with excitement. He never knew whether she understood everything he said, but he talked to her as if she did, and she wriggled like a puppy. After a few minutes, he gently lowered her paws off his leg and wheeled the bike up beside the garage. Then he cocked his head. From the barn, he caught the *skritch-skritch* of a brush. Sure enough, Brenin appeared at the barn door. The alpha cŵn looked at Ricky before retreating inside.

Inside the horse barn, Ricky found Ioan brushing his mount. Ioan looked over and smiled, set down the brush and wordlessly came over to put an arm around Ricky in a half embrace.

Ioan asked how the trip had gone, and he seemed genuinely interested in the answers, genuinely happy to have Ricky back. The truth, Ricky was certain, was that Ioan *was* interested, was happy. The question he couldn't answer, and maybe never would, maybe never should, was *why*.

Ricky was the Cŵn Annwn's Arawn. That gave their pack power. It also gave them leverage with Matilda. Ricky would champion them with her, and as long as his bond with Liv remained strong, so would hers with the Huntsmen. It was in Ioan's best interests to make nice. If Ricky felt that his interest went beyond that, was that his ego talking? Not wanting to think Ioan and the pack treated him well only because he was useful as Arawn?

It wasn't dissimilar from his situation with the Saints. Everyone knew his father intended to make him leader, and as long as he lived up to his potential—which he was doing—he'd assume the mantle in about ten years. So it was in each member's best interest to treat Ricky well, securing *their* future position. With both the Cŵn Annwn and the Saints, Ricky could accept that and use it to his advantage and not give a shit about things like genuine friendship, genuine belonging. Except he wasn't that guy. Never would be. He wanted the biker life too much, and he needed it to want him back. Same with the Cŵn Annwn.

No matter how different the groups might seem, they were at their heart the same, with their sense of camaraderie and purpose, and Ricky loved being a Huntsman as much as he loved being a biker. Most times, he accepted that he did fit. Their attention and affection felt genuine, and so it was, and the rest was navel-gazing overanalysis. There were still, though, moments when his mood dipped, and he couldn't help but wonder whether he was like the guy who got accepted into the cool clique in high school because he had a nice car or a fat bank account.

Ioan was also Ricky's grandfather. Ricky preferred to forget that part. It added a layer of awkwardness that didn't help reconcile his ambivalence. Ioan played the role of the proud grandfather, thrilled by Ricky's accomplishments, pleased by the man he'd become, and all of that seemed sincere. Good, right? His grandfather had entered his life, and now they could have the relationship that had been denied them. Only it hadn't been denied them at all.

Ioan had gotten Ricky's grandmother pregnant when she was a young woman, and then he'd left, acknowledging Ricky's father only with punctual and very generous support checks. What Ioan did doomed Ricky's grandmother to life as an ostracized single mother. Not that Ricky would ever say that to her face. She'd tell him off if he did. To her, that baby and those checks meant she could open her own business and never need to marry, enjoying lovers instead. Still, Ricky knew that part of that had been his strong-willed grandmother making the best of difficult circumstances. Making lemonade from the lemons Ioan had given her.

For Ioan to waltz into Ricky's life and see no problem with what he'd done? That burned. Ricky had eventually told Ioan how much it burned, what a shitty thing it'd been to do, and he knew that'd been a revelation to Ioan. Airing that issue had helped, but it didn't fix the past, and Ricky had come to accept that he might always prefer to simply think of Ioan as "leader of the Cŵn Annwn." A colleague, a mentor, maybe even someday a friend, but nothing more.

They finished the small talk, and then Ricky headed through the airy stable to where his horse, Tywysog Du, had an oversized stall. All the stalls here were huge, with acres of pasture beyond and two Huntsmen assigned as full-time staff. Like the hounds, the horses weren't pets or property. They were partners, treated with all due respect. It didn't matter that there was a Huntsman on duty in the stable even now—Ioan would be here every morning before work to curry his horse and put him out for the day.

Ricky brought Tywysog Du from his stall and led him over near Ioan. Then he picked up a currycomb and began working his way down from the horse's neck.

"The body is Kirkman's," Ricky said as he circled the comb over Tywysog Du's flank.

Ioan shook his head. "That isn't possible."

"Gabriel was there. The police were following an anonymous call. They found Kirkman's last victim in the brush where he left her. They found him buried right beside her."

"Which means it's not Gregory Kirkman. I realize Liv is worried, and if she's worried, then you are. Overreaction is completely understandable under the—"

"Ioan?"

That was all Ricky said. Just the one word and an accompanying look. Ioan nodded and murmured an apology. Liv and Gabriel dealt with the same crap from the elders. The leaders of the Tylwyth

Teg and the Cŵn Annwn saw them as children and needed to be constantly reminded that they weren't, and that patronizing "I understand your concern" bullshit was not appreciated.

If Ricky were a two-hundred-year-old fae, he'd probably treat a twenty-something human the same way. That didn't mean Ricky had to put up with it. So he didn't, and he had to give Ioan props for acknowledging his mistakes, something Liv and Gabriel never got from the elders.

"It's the body of a man," Ricky said. "Roughly the same age as Kirkman. Buried for about twenty years. The remains showing signs of a savage knife attack. And he had Kirkman's ID on him."

"There," Ioan said with satisfaction, turning from his horse. "That last part proves this is not Gregory Kirkman. I destroyed his ID myself. All the contents of his wallet are gone."

"This was a social security card."

Ioan paused. "He didn't have that on him. I emptied his pockets. Two Huntsmen searched him after me to be sure. It's standard procedure. The card on that body was planted."

"Yes."

Ioan stopped, as if he'd been about to argue.

"We figured that," Ricky said. "Whoever moved him wanted to make sure he was ID'd. They found or made a social security card to point the cops in the right direction."

"Or the wrong direction, if it's not Kirkman."

Ricky switched the currycomb for the dandy brush. "Yeah, that might have worked fifty years ago. We have forensics now. They won't positively ID him as Kirkman until they're sure he is."

"Whoever moved him might not know that. Or they might not care. I don't think anyone is trying to put Todd back in prison. They're simply raising the possibility. I know this will sound like blame shifting, but the most likely suspect is a fae who wants something from Liv or Gabriel."

"Yeah, we figured that out, too. And sure, there's a chance this isn't Kirkman. But put the pieces together. Guy about his age, dead about as long as he was, buried beside the body of his victim. He was never arrested for those crimes."

"The police did investigate him."

Ricky set down the brush. "You don't want us second-guessing your work, so you're going to deny the possibility this could be Kirkman, and therefore block us from preparing in case it is."

"I'm not—"

"Levi's jeans. Work boots. Red plaid lumberman's jacket. Black T-shirt."

Ioan went still, and Ricky knew this matched his memory of Greg Kirkman. However many souls the Cŵn Annwn reaped, they remembered each one. Those deaths didn't haunt them. Didn't bother them at all—they knew beyond a shadow of a doubt that their targets were guilty, and they had complete faith in the righteousness of their actions. No, the dead were merely index cards in their mental filing cabinets. Cards that could be pulled forth at a moment's notice.

Ioan opened his mouth, and Ricky slapped the brush onto the table. "Forget it, okay? Just forget it."

"I didn't say anything, Ricky."

"You were about to point out that whoever did this might have dressed the corpse to match. Might *somehow* have known what Kirkman was wearing and set the stage. Though, even as you said that, you'd be remembering who else had that information. Todd, yes, but also Liv, who saw it last year in Todd's memories. She could have given me that to pass on to you if you refused to believe it was

Kirkman. Of course, you know better than to accuse Liv of tricking you, so you'll stick with 'maybe this body was dressed to match.'"

Ioan didn't protest. Didn't say Ricky was wrong.

"I'm not accusing you of anything," Ricky said. "The sluagh set this whole Kirkman thing up. Just tell me that she knew where the body was, and we can start looking at her followers."

"She didn't. That's the problem. No one else knew..." Ioan trailed off. Then he cleared his throat. "We took the body. Wmffre and I. We buried it while the others stood watch. Wmffre..." A pause, and Ricky nodded—the Huntsman had been killed by the sluagh.

Ioan continued. "I'm certain he told no one. That leaves me."

"And who else?"

"No one—"

"You were about to say no one else knew, and then you stopped. You remembered someone else had been there."

"It's nothing I can prove."

Ricky walked around Tywysog Du and faced Ioan. "I don't care about proof. This isn't accusing someone. It's giving us a direction to search."

"Yes, but if it's not a direction Liv..." He took a deep breath. "Someone else was there. Someone was watching. We never realized it at the time. Neither did Todd. Only Liv did, when she saw his memory. Someone was there, and she figured out who it must have been. The only person who knew what Todd had done. The one who heard me make him the offer, and then came to me, supposedly on his behalf, to accept that offer. The one who killed those six people for us."

"Fuck," Ricky breathed. "You mean..."

Ioan nodded. "Pamela."

THIRTEEN

OLIVIA

GABRIEL WAS gone, talking to the elders. Giving them shit, really, but in that very Gabriel-way where, to an outsider, it sounded like a conversation...yet if you were on the receiving end, you knew exactly what it was. Every ten minutes, like clockwork, I'd get a text from him with a single word.

No.

That word had nothing to do with the elders. It was in answer to a question I hadn't asked. One he knew I was asking, constantly, in my head.

Has anyone contacted you yet?

Has anyone sent you an article on Kirkman? An e-mail. A text? A voice mail? Have they dropped it off at the office? Had it delivered there? The fact that Cainsville had secured its perimeter meant our fae adversary couldn't drop off a copy of the newspaper on our front porch. They also couldn't do it at Gabriel's high-security condo—not easily, at least. If they wanted an actual copy of the article delivered, with no electronic way of tracking the sender, they'd drop it off at the office. Lydia had been asked to contact me at home in the event of any delivery, even if the package seemed to come from a client. Same for any calls, e-mails, faxes… Hey, fae were old. They might still fax.

It was ten a.m., and no one had made contact. The unearthing had hit the news. Kirkman had even been nonpositively ID'd—someone on the force had leaked his social security card to the media, who reported that the dead man appeared to be Gregory Kirkman, a construction worker who'd disappeared twenty-five years ago, and who'd lived near the burial site.

The articles, however, focused more on the young woman. Kirkman's final victim. Three others had been discovered before her, and when the police investigated, they hadn't tied this fourth missing girl to the same killer. The girl in the deadfall. The girl the Cŵn Annwn had left there, in the expectation someone would find her, and her family would have closure. That hadn't happened. Now they had that, and she had a name: Laura Simmons.

The papers, rightfully, focused on her story. Unlike the other three, she'd been a runaway, which was why her "disappearance" had never been connected to the other three. Apparently, Kirkman had realized it would be easier to snatch girls whose parents didn't expect them home at night. He'd escalated in his sadism, too. The first two girls had been raped and strangled. The third had suffered more, but it was nothing compared to what Todd remembered from seeing Laura Simmons's body under the deadfall. Fortunately for her family, no signs of her ordeal remained. It existed only in my memories, in my nightmares. I'd keep it there—I could deal with it better than her loved ones could.

The reason the papers focused on Laura, though, was that they had no reason to think Kirkman was connected in any way. The police *had* considered him a suspect in the murders. A strong one.

Then he'd disappeared. When no other suspects arose for the case, the police had officially left it open but internally considered it closed, their suspect dead or long gone.

At the time, to the general public, the bodies of two teens had been found, raped and strangled, and that certainly screamed serial killer, but before victim three was even found, another case took over the headlines—the Valentine Killer. The ritualistic murder of four couples. Those poor girls and their killer faded into obscurity as soon as experts concluded they weren't also Valentine Killer victims.

Now, with the discovery of Laura Simmons, journalists had dug into their old files and unearthed stories of Kirkman's first two victims and the third body discovered later. That gave them something almost as interesting as an active serial killer: a cold case file.

Did anyone tie those deaths to the Valentine Killer? Of course they did, as they had back then. But every article I read referenced older ones and agreed this was a separate case. Strangulation in both, yes. But no signs of ritualism with the first set, and no signs of sexual assault with the second. Those first four fit a far more common serial killer pattern—the degradation and murder of teenage girls.

I'd been up at six, reading every article, looking for a link to my father. I didn't dare search on Gregory Kirkman plus Todd Larsen. No matter how secure my laptop was supposed to be, I'd never risk linking them in my search history. So I read the articles. Two mentioned Todd, but only in connection with the potential Valentine Killer link. In the context of: *yes, these deaths occurred right before the murderous spree of the notorious Valentine Killer—the crimes for which Todd Larsen was recently acquitted—but experts agree the cases are not linked.* His name was invoked only in passing, a way to tie these old crimes to more recent headlines.

As for Kirkman, his body barely warranted a footnote in the articles. "Police also uncovered the body of a man believed to be long-missing Illinois construction worker Gregory Kirkman." One article speculated on a connection between Kirkman and Laura Simmons, but only by raising the possibility Kirkman was another victim of Laura's killer, maybe having been an unwitting witness to her death, given that he lived so close to the crime scene.

This was all good. All what I would expect. I also expected, though, that whoever moved Kirkman's body would alert me to these articles. Yet it was late morning, and no one had.

Gabriel texted to say he was finished with the elders. They were convinced I'd just seen a curious face as Pepper suggested. Grace hadn't been there. He wanted to speak to her next. I debated telling him to skip it. The farther I got from last night, the more I questioned my own sense of events. I'd been on edge and looking for trouble, expecting trouble. Fae *were* curious beings. Some subtypes were also skittish. As much as I hated to admit it, this explanation made sense. A local fae had spotted Todd walking and talking to Ricky and wondered what Matilda's father and Arawn would talk about. She slipped into her camouflaged state and snuck up on them, and she'd been so engrossed in their interaction that I startled her. She gave me a fae-powered shove and fled.

I sent the text. Gabriel replied in seconds, saying he understood, but he thought it wise to meet with Grace anyway. He'd seen her heading to the diner.

You could join us for coffee, he texted. *Bring your father to meet her.*

My fingers hovered over my phone, ready to type back that Todd had met Grace. That wasn't exactly true. I just didn't want to leave the house, in case…

In case what? It was extremely unlikely that anyone would deliver news of Kirkman's unearthing to my front door. I had my phone set to check for mail every five minutes, polling both my personal and work accounts. I'd finished reading all the morning articles. Todd was out back, going a little stir-crazy, I suspected.

I texted Gabriel: *Be there in 10. Pie?*

He sent back a list of the daily offerings as I called to Todd from the back door. When Todd didn't respond, my heart double-thudded, and I stepped out with a sharp, "Dad?"

He appeared from underneath the back deck. I laughed as he brushed dirt from his jeans.

"Dare I ask what you were doing under there?" I said.

"Checking the foundation. It's fine, but whoever built this deck did a crap job."

"Like I said, we're tearing it down soon. Gabriel is looking for a contractor. He's very, very picky." Speaking of Gabriel... "What kind of pie do you like? Options are blueberry, strawberry rhubarb and lemon meringue."

"For lunch?"

"Second coffee break. Gabriel's at the diner with one of the elders you should meet, and he's preordering pie."

"I'll take the—"

A rap sounded at the gate. As I jogged over, I could see someone in a uniform. Like a delivery driver. Ah, so, that's how they were doing it—sending the article by courier. I picked up my pace and swung open the gate.

"Hey," I said, putting out my hand for the envelope.

That's when I saw the uniforms. They weren't couriers.

The woman stepped forward. "Ms. Jones? We'd like to speak to your father about the murder of Gregory Kirkman."

FOURTEEN

OLIVIA

I DID not politely usher Detective Parsons and her partner into the house so they could speak to my father. Hell, no. I flipped into full-out bitch socialite mode. How dare you come to my house and interrogate my father less than forty-eight hours after he's been released from prison. Don't you people have real crimes to solve? How about finding the actual Valentine Killer, for a start. Now you have a twenty-year-old corpse, and the first person you question is my father? Is that what his life is going to be like now? The police are going to hound him into a nervous breakdown?

That wasn't fair. Not a single word of it. First, I liked Detective Parsons, and I knew she was an excellent detective who had nothing to do with putting my father in prison. According to Gabriel, she'd actually been on Todd's side.

Then there was the small fact that my father *did* commit this particular crime. That was why I pulled the full drama queen routine. I had to act exactly like they'd expect if he were innocent. Shocked and appalled and outraged.

Even as I reamed them out, I was texting Gabriel. I made it clear that, as furious as I was, I wasn't interfering with their interrogation—there was no reason to do that when my father was innocent of this frivolous and malicious accusation—but I was making damned sure Gabriel was here in case they tried to intimidate Todd into a false confession.

Gabriel showed up and gave them round two of outrage and, in his case, *quiet* fury. Everything I'd said, he repeated, in clipped, precise language. Unacceptable. Completely unacceptable, and while he would allow the questioning, it had better not be a sign of sustained harassment to come.

As for Todd, he stood to one side and listened and said nothing. His expression betrayed only quiet resignation, as one might expect to see on a life-sentence convict who has been acquitted. Not even a flicker of guilt crossed his face.

We went inside. Parsons hadn't said much during either lecture. Her younger partner had bristled, but she'd kept him in check with pointed looks. Only when we went inside did she say, quietly and calmly, "You know if we receive a tip, we have to follow it up, Gabriel. I realize this seems unfair, but be glad it's me doing it."

"I would prefer no one did it at all," Gabriel said.

"So would I."

We led them into the parlor, where everyone sat.

"You said you had a lead," I began. "Let me guess. You found a twenty-five-year-old corpse and someone called Crime Stoppers saying 'Todd Larsen did it!'"

Parsons looked from me to Gabriel.

Gabriel said, "Olivia has every right to be present for this interview. She is my investigator."

"Right now, I think she's wearing her daughter hat."

"Possibly. Feel free to tell her to leave. Given that it's her house, though, she won't go far. She'll lurk right outside the door and interject her opinions as needed, which I'm sure you'll find far less intrusive."

Parsons sighed and glanced at me. "I know this is a pain in the ass. Let's just get through it, okay?"

"That's what I was doing," I said.

"With added color commentary." She turned to Todd. "Are you aware that a body was uncovered yesterday?"

Todd nodded. "Gabriel mentioned it at dinner. He was there as the landowner's attorney. A guy and a girl, right? A couple? Is that the connection?"

"You have been acquitted—" Gabriel began.

"Yeah, I know," Todd said. "Which doesn't mean everyone agrees I should have been. If the police find the bodies of a couple killed twenty-five years ago, they're going to come to me. I expect that."

"You shouldn't," I grumbled.

Parsons continued. "We found a male and a female corpse, but there's no connection between them. The connection, as our anonymous caller informed us, is between you and the male victim. A man named Gregory Kirkman."

"Gregory..."

"Kirkman."

Todd went quiet, as if thinking. "Was he in prison with me?"

"No, he disappeared two years before your arrest."

"Someone I knew before then? The name's not ringing a bell. Is he from my school days?"

"Later. After you married and had Oliv—Eden. He was a friend of yours."

"Friend?" Todd gave a short laugh and settled back in his seat. "I was twenty-one years old with a wife, baby and mortgage. The only thing I did in those days was work."

"You were a carpenter. Mr. Kirkman was a construction worker. Maybe 'friend' is an exaggeration. You worked on a job together."

"Okay…"

"His crew was renovating a house, and you came in to do the cupboards."

Todd shrugged. "If you say so. I'm not denying it. But I was a self-employed carpenter. I went where the work was. I couldn't tell you how many guys I worked with, and even then, it was me making cupboards and such at my shop, and then coming to install them while the renovators did their thing. I talked to some of the guys, but I didn't hang out after the job and have a beer with them. I had Pam and Eden." He nodded toward me. "Liv."

"If you have read the transcripts from Todd's original trial, then you know what he's saying is documented fact," Gabriel said. "He was a hardworking husband and father with little time for socializing. A positive trait that was twisted against him in court, implying he was a loner who fit the stereotypical profile of a serial killer, when in fact—"

"Mortgage, wife, baby," Parsons said. "I know."

She took out a photograph. I recognized Kirkman in a heartbeat. Fortunately, her gaze stayed on Todd, who only frowned at it. He reached out, and she passed it over.

"Honestly, he looks like half the construction guys I knew," Todd said. "I don't…" He paused in the midst of handing it back and withdrew it for another look. "Wait. Was it a job in Hyde Park? No, Barrington, right? Cupboards for a total home reno? I was there for a couple of days. If this is the guy I'm thinking of, he did talk to me. He was building a place himself. He had a few questions about joints. I think that was him. I don't even remember his name, though. It was just a couple of conversations while I worked. He held the cupboards in place for me."

"Mr. Kirkman was indeed building his own home," Parsons said. "The caller, however, implied there was a deeper connection between you and Mr. Kirkman. He said that you met on that job and then started meeting in secret. It stood out as unusually social behavior for you *and* for Mr. Kirkman, which apparently led to rumors among the crew of…" She cleared her throat. "An intimate relationship."

"What?" Todd said. "Uh, no. On all counts. No, I did not ever meet this Kirkman guy in secret for any purpose. And no, there *weren't* rumors like that. I'd have heard them. Guys don't just whisper that behind your back. *Someone's* going to say it to your face."

"Todd is correct," Gabriel said. "It is indeed the sort of rumor that men—particularly in that time period and that job environment—would say aloud. What you have, Detective, is clearly an informant who wishes to cause trouble. My suggestion would be to take a closer look at Mr. Kirkman's coworkers. Those who worked as part of his team rather than, like Todd, only incidentally."

"We—"

Gabriel continued. "Whoever notified you of Mr. Kirkman's body was aware of his connection—however tenuous—with Todd. That suggests a coworker. It also, as you must be aware, means that this informant knew where to find Mr. Kirkman's body, which makes him a prime suspect for the murder. This person kills his coworker. Later, he sees Todd in the news and realizes they'd met on a job, that Mr. Kirkman knew a convicted serial killer. Mr. Kirkman's murderer decides to plant an identification card. The fact it's a social security card strengthens the work connection—someone who employed Mr. Kirkman would know that number and could create a fake card.

When Todd is acquitted, the murderer decides—perhaps tired of worrying about Mr. Kirkman being discovered—to lead police to his body and inform them of the link between him and Todd."

"Thank you, Gabriel," Parsons said. "You've solved our crime for us."

"Hardly," Gabriel said, ignoring her sarcasm. "You still need to find the person who placed the anonymous tip. However, if I may speculate further, you should consider their link to the young woman found nearby. That is not coincidental. I'm sure you realize that."

Parsons said nothing.

"I saw this morning that police were connecting her to several other murders," Gabriel said. "Ones that first came to my attention in Todd's case file. The unsolved murders of three young women. One of those was also found in the forest adjoining Mr. Kirkman's property. Was he ever investigated for the crime?"

Parsons turned to Todd. "Mr. Larsen—"

"Todd, please. I've finally broken Gabriel of that." He offered a faint smile.

"All right. Todd. Is there anything you can tell us that would help clear you of these allegations?"

"Like an alibi? When was he killed?"

She gave a date and said, "That was the last time Mr. Kirkman was seen. He left Chicago after having drinks with several colleagues, and he didn't return to work the next day."

"Well, if it was a weekday, presumably, then I'd have been at work until maybe six. After that, I'd have gone home for dinner. I might have worked more in the evening, or I could have been with Pam and Eden."

Gabriel cleared his throat. "It's been twenty-five years. There is no way of determining time of death with any accuracy, so even if

Todd could provide an ironclad alibi for the night of Mr. Kirkman's disappearance, it would mean nothing."

"I know." Parsons sighed and looked at her partner, who shrugged, having nothing to add.

"There is one more thing," she said.

She read off a phone number. Recognition sparked in Todd's eyes, and his mouth started to open. Then he glanced at Gabriel. "That sounds like…"

"Your old phone number?" Parsons said.

Todd smiled, a seemingly genuine one. "Yeah. I'm amazed I remember it."

"That number was found in Mr. Kirkman's pocket. Written on the back of a business card. *Your* business card, Todd. Your business number was on the front, but you'd written your personal one on the back."

"Yes," Gabriel said. "I believe my client already admitted he'd been answering construction questions—"

"Are you leading the witness, counselor?" Parsons asked.

"I thought he was a suspect."

"Gabriel…" Parsons warned. "This crap might work with newbies, but remember who you're speaking to." She turned to her partner. "Take note, Jim. In saying that, Mr. Walsh was providing his client with a potential excuse for the card."

"He doesn't need to," Todd said. "I would love to see what I got for a business card. Was it a nice one?"

Parsons's brows knitted.

"Sorry, Detective," Todd said. "I don't mean to make light. The thing is that I never had cards. That was a private joke between me and Pam. She thought I should have them, and I kept picking out cute designs with cartoon hammers and whatever. She wanted the professional-looking ones. I thought they were boring…and expensive, with embossing and foil and all that. So I never got cards. I didn't need them, really. Not to brag, but people saw my work and looked me up."

"We would still like to see that card," I said. "It might contain clues."

"You're not investigating this, Liv," Parsons said. "It's police work."

"If it involves my father, I'm investigating it," I said. "And, if Gabriel's right, the person who accused my father might also be Mr. Kirkman's killer. Consider it free private eye work. Save some money on your budget."

She rolled her eyes but didn't comment. The interview wound down after that, and I hoped that would be the end of it. The evidence they had was circumstantial, and Gabriel and my father had explained it away nicely. Still…

We presumed this was a fae trying to get our attention. Alerting us to the body? That was reasonable. But calling the police? Planting that business card on Kirkman's body? It was too much for an idle threat. Far too much.

FIFTEEN

OLIVIA

RICKY HAD texted, wanting to stop in and discuss his talk with Ioan. I figured he didn't have anything for me since he didn't text until hours after he visited Ioan. I said I'd be around. Gabriel had left for the office, and I was left twiddling my thumbs, telling myself everything was okay while knowing it wasn't.

Todd was out back when Ricky arrived. I heard the rumble of the Harley and met him in the driveway. We went inside before exchanging more than small talk.

"You okay?" I asked as I took his jacket.

He shrugged, which meant no, he wasn't. I didn't prod. He'd speak when he was ready. Or he wouldn't, which would mean the problem was work-related, and I *couldn't* prod about that.

"Have you eaten?" I asked.

He shook his head, and I took him into the kitchen where the remains of lunch still covered the counter. Cold cuts, cheeses, rolls, pickles and salads. He fixed himself a sandwich. As he was closing the roll, I said, "Going vegetarian?"

"Hmm?"

I pointed at the bun, with lettuce, cheese, tomatoes and condiments. It took him a moment to see what I meant. Then, without a word, he piled on his usual mountain of cold cuts and carried his plate to the table.

"Have you heard anything?" he asked. "From whoever tipped off the cops?"

I grabbed a soda from the fridge for him and popped it open. In this state, he'd probably forget to do that and spend his meal wondering why he wasn't getting anything from the can.

I told him what had happened. I didn't get farther than "The police suspected Todd," before he snapped out of his distraction. I had his full attention for the rest.

"Shit," he said when I finished.

"Yep. We're lucky it's Detective Parsons, or my father might be back in a jail cell right now."

"That's bullshit," he said. "Okay, yeah, I know—this is the one thing your dad actually did. But I don't care. Kirkman deserved the death penalty, and even if a court would have found Todd guilty, he's served his time."

"It doesn't work like that."

"It should." He pushed aside his plate, sandwich untouched. "Hell, Todd should be able to come right out and say, 'Yep, I did it. I stopped a serial killer before he took any more victims, and I don't regret it, and I served my time, so the slate is clear.' He doesn't deserve this. Your mother set him up before and now…"

He trailed off.

"For now, he's safe," I said. "Gabriel gave them a good alternate theory. A really good one. We also got information that will help us solve this. Whoever did it knew Kirkman worked with my father.

They planted both the social security card and a fake business card. This is a fae who's working very hard to get our attention. One who wants to make the threat as serious as possible. I underestimated them. They're not content with threatening to link Todd to this crime. They already have. Which means they have more evidence, and that's what they'll threaten us with. Do what I want, or I'll turn this over to the police."

Ricky said nothing.

I continued. "Gabriel's tracking down that lead right now. Detective Parsons wouldn't give us much, of course, but she's letting Gabriel see the business card and the social security one. He thinks he might also have a contact who'll get him that anonymous tip—the recording and any associated information. Anonymous only means you don't leave your name. There's still data there. It'll cost, but I'll pay whatever it takes to get a lead on this fae bastard."

"Are you sure it's a fae?"

I was at the counter, tidying up while snacking on the leftovers. I looked over at him, a pickle slice at my lips.

He repeated the question.

"It has to be, doesn't it?" I said. "Only fae can connect my father to Kirkman. The Cŵn Annwn or the sluagh. They were both directly involved, and only they'd know where to find the body. Even if a human did, I'm only useful to fae. Same as you or Gabriel. Well, no, obviously we have other roles, but no one's going to do this because they want to get into the Saints or they want Gabriel to take their legal case."

I paused. "If it was human, it'd be about money. I have that from my inheritance. But that loops back to the problem of a human finding out—both that Todd did it and where the body was buried. Even Todd himself didn't know the last part."

"Someone else might have."

He said it quietly, as if afraid to raise the possibility. That made me stop and look at him. Ricky never hesitates to raise an idea. Gabriel or I might. We're the kids who won't raise our hands with a potentially stupid question. Ricky has no such qualms. He'll put it out there with a disclaimer—"I know this might sound stupid"—but he still mentions it, as he should. Fear of looking foolish keeps us from thinking more creatively, spitballing and brainstorming our way to answers.

So when he hesitated here, so did I. He wasn't afraid of pushing the possibility this wasn't fae. There was something about the question that he was reluctant to voice.

Before I could ask, he waved for me to sit. I did.

"Ioan says the sluagh didn't know where he buried Kirkman," he said. "She wasn't there at the time, and she never asked. She was completely disinterested in Greg Kirkman and his case."

"He was a means to an end."

He nodded. "Even most of the Huntsmen didn't know where exactly to find the body. Ioan buried it along with Wmffre."

"Who died as a loyal Huntsman, helping us, which means he is extremely unlikely to have ever talked about Kirkman's burial spot."

"Right."

"That leaves Ioan, who *wouldn't* talk about it. There's absolutely no point in that."

Ricky said nothing.

"You think Ioan did?" I asked.

"No, like you said, there's no advantage to it. But when you say that leaves him as the only person who knew..." He took a deep breath. "Ioan pointed out another possibility, and I should have come straight here after he did. I've been working it through, trying to prove him wrong, so I didn't have to raise the possibility."

"What possibility?"

"Someone else was there that night," he said. "With Todd and Kirkman. Todd suspected it. You figured it out. We just...we all forgot that part."

"Who...?"

I trailed off. And then I remembered.

SIXTEEN

OLIVIA

I WAS in the prison. Not the one my father had just been released from, but one I knew equally well. Ricky had taken the afternoon off, and he was working from our place while "hanging out" with Todd—a nice way of saying he was babysitting my father.

I waited in a private visiting room. When the door opened, I'd have loved to have been feigning interest in my cell phone as an excuse to not look up right away. But my phone was in the car. Otherwise, I'd have had to hand it in. So I sat with my hands folded on the small desk, and when my mother walked in, I had to look up.

After my father had been acquitted, half the online comments were from people who supposedly always thought he was innocent. They could tell, just by looking at him, that he wasn't a killer, and twenty-three years in prison hadn't changed that. What they meant was that he didn't look like a monster. He was a good-looking guy with an open face and an easy smile. Nothing harsh or even hard about him.

The early photographs of my mother had gotten a very different reaction. It wasn't a guilt-ridden expression or haunted eyes. Just the opposite. There'd been a toughness in Pamela Larsen that rubbed people the wrong way. A defiance. A self-confidence. Terribly unbecoming in a young woman. And while she was attractive enough, people had found her wanting compared to my father. He was a solid eight, and she was maybe a seven, and if the gender roles had been reversed, that would have been fine, but it didn't seem right for guys to date downward on the scale. Believe me, I'd gotten my share of that when I'd dated Ricky.

Now, though, Gabriel made sure that any article on Pamela's case included an updated photo of her. A prison photo, one where she slacked her perfect posture and hid the steel in her eyes. Without those, she looked like a pleasant middle-aged woman. She'd put on thirty or forty pounds in prison, which took the edge off her figure, quite literally. It softened and rounded her, and when she gave just the right smile, a little bit shy, a little bit uncertain—and totally fake—you couldn't believe such a woman killed anyone.

Today, Pamela wasn't getting a photo taken, so when she walked in, her posture was military straight, her eyes expressionless. A woman who dared you to underestimate her. When I saw my mother like this, my heart ached with wishing things could be different between us. This was a mother I could be proud of. A mother I could learn from. A mother who was everything I wanted. Yet Pamela had done things that meant we could never have that relationship, and if she'd done what I now suspected her of, this would be the last time I saw her. I would make sure of that.

When she spotted me, those eyes softened. She smiled. Not her fake smile of harmless maternal affection. We were long past that charade. Instead, I got a smile of pride and *her* kind of maternal affection—fierce and unyielding and dangerous to anyone who crossed it. She looked at me the way I wanted to look at her.

"Eden," she said and gave me a quick embrace, the guard knowing better than to do more than clear her throat at it.

My mother turned and nodded, and the guard retreated to her corner. Well trained. Probably well compensated. Since Pamela had become the mother of Matilda, fae courted her favor, and however much she hated their kind, she was not above using them. Any guard susceptible to bribery would find Pamela Larsen had developed a network of wealthy and influential benefactors.

"Have you been watching the news?" I asked as we sat.

"Considering that your father was just released from prison, I've decided to take a break from television and newspapers."

"Because he's out there, and you're in here?"

A flash of what seemed like genuine confusion. Then another flash, annoyance at me for being so petty. "Of course not. If the media wishes to congratulate him on his release, then I'm glad for it. He deserves that. But I'm sure there are far less congratulatory mentions of his release, and I do *not* need to see those."

I studied her expression.

"What's wrong?" she said.

When I didn't answer right away, she said, "Something is wrong, and it's related to your father's release and—shockingly—you think I've done something."

"Shockingly...because you never do anything."

Her expression stayed neutral. "Eden, what's happening?"

"Last year, I gave you a name. One Seanna passed to me."

She didn't say the name. She knew better with the guard in the room. She only nodded for me to continue.

"Someone dug into the past," I said. "Quite literally."

Her brows knitted for only a second. Then she said, "He's been...?"

"Yes. An anonymous call led the police to him. The same call sent them to my front door this morning wanting to speak to Todd."

She swore under her breath. "Tylwyth Teg. It must be. Or other fae."

We didn't bother to hide this part of the conversation. If the guard could overhear, she'd think she was mistaken.

"Not Cŵn Annwn?" I asked.

A dismissive wave. "No. They held up their end of the deal. They've made mistakes, but honest ones, which they've rectified. You might call them fae, but they're not. I have no issue with the Cŵn Annwn. This is fae."

She sank into her thoughts for a minute. Then she went still and looked up sharply. "You think *I'm* the anonymous caller?"

Before I could answer, her face darkened, eyes snapping. "I would never hurt your father like that."

I raised my brows. It was all I had to do. Her cheeks flushed. "We agreed on that. He insisted. You know it."

She meant that my father insisted they go to prison together. It'd been presumed that Pamela hadn't acted alone. She was a woman—of course she'd had a man guiding her, if not outright forcing her to commit these atrocities. To avoid sharing her fate, my father would have needed to turn on her. Prove that she'd acted alone. If he'd done that, she wouldn't have had any chance of freedom.

If it were Gabriel and I, and I'd committed the crime, he might make the same choice...and I wouldn't let him. I'd confess. Pamela hadn't done that, and so I hold her responsible. My father doesn't see it that way. She executed six murderers to cure me. He'd executed one to contact the Cŵn Annwn in hopes of winning that cure. To him, their crimes are equal. I agree. They are equally forgivable. But the arrest had been for her crimes, not his, and so she should have spared him the punishment, taken her chances with the court and left me my father.

She leaned across the table. "I would not hurt him. I want him free. You know that, Eden. I told you that I would do whatever it took to get him free for you, and you decided against that route. You trusted Gabriel. Gabriel won your father's release, and so anything I had against your lover is gone. He got your father out for you. I would do nothing to change that. I wouldn't hurt either of you that way."

She was right. She had offered to confess if it would get Todd out. That didn't mean, though, that there wasn't some deeper machination at work here, some angle she was playing.

"You say it's fae," I said.

She straightened, relaxing. "Yes. That's the obvious answer."

"So who?"

"How would I—?"

"That night, there were three parties present. Only three. Todd. The Hunt. And one onlooker, unseen by either of them. One who, as you know, I saw. One who has confessed she was there."

She went still. "Yes, but—"

"You followed my father. He'd been distracted, and when he said he had to work late, you feared he was having an affair. You followed him. You saw how he…handled the situation, and you overheard his conversation with Ioan. You knew about the deal, and when he didn't follow up on it, you did. You pretended he'd asked you to deal with Ioan for safety—to put more distance between himself and the crimes. Ioan thought he was communicating with Todd through you."

"Yes. To all of that."

"Which means you are the only other person who knew about it. Knew how Todd handled it. Knew how Ioan handled it. *Where* he handled it."

"Where—?" Her gaze cut to the guard, who was busy checking her phone, paying no apparent attention to us. Pamela said, with care, "If you mean that I knew where to find that which was hidden, I did not. As soon as Todd spoke to Ioan, I left. Quickly. I needed to pick you up at my mother's and get home before your father did. I couldn't let him know I'd been gone. So the moment I heard what I needed to, I left."

I shook my head. "You didn't need to rush. Todd had to...clean up. It would take time."

"Which I did not realize."

I remembered Todd's enraged attack. "How couldn't you? If you saw what happened—"

"I *didn't* see it. I was coming through the forest when I heard them talking. I stopped to listen. It was over before I got close enough to see anything, and I didn't want to. I didn't need to. I hid in the forest while I tried to figure out what to do. That's when the Hunt came. As soon as I heard Ioan's offer, I left. Check the timing with your father and with Ioan. It didn't take Todd long to return home. When he did, you were sound asleep, and I had food ready for him. A hot snack and a cold beer. Unless I can be in two places at once, Eden, I didn't see where anything was hidden. I presume Ioan took his time with that. By the time they were doing it, Todd was probably already home. Check with them."

"You didn't hang back, Mom. Todd heard you. Right there."

"He never said—"

"He thought he heard something in the bushes. He dismissed it. When I was there, in his memory, I heard two rustles close by."

"I never got within twenty feet of them, Eden. I could see flashlights through the trees. Flashlight beams and shapes. That's it."

I patted my pockets and found a receipt crumpled in the bottom of one. I tore it up to draw a map on the tabletop, indicating the figures in question and pointing out the directions and the nearest roads.

"We came in here," she said, pointing. "I was following far enough behind your father that he wouldn't see me. He was on his bicycle. I was in the car with the lights off. It took me a while to catch up—I thought I'd lost him until I heard voices."

In Todd's memory, he'd heard the bushes crackle before Kirkman arrived. Yet it did make sense—Pamela *couldn't* have followed that closely.

She pointed out the rough route she took, and where she'd hidden. It was on the opposite side of where I'd heard someone. Which meant that whoever was there? It wasn't Pamela.

SEVENTEEN

OLIVIA

GABRIEL AND I were in the forest, standing in the spot where the bodies had been found. The police had finished their work, the area empty but still marked with crime scene tape and easy to find. It was still possible they'd return, maybe even as we stood here. If so, we had a ready alibi—someone was framing Todd, and we'd told Detective Parsons we'd be investigating.

I'd come in hopes of getting a vision, maybe revisiting the one with Todd the night he killed Kirkman. So far, I hadn't seen even a flicker.

"It doesn't make logical sense for someone else to have been here," I said as I paced. "Two people following Todd? No. We know Pamela was here. She's lying to cover it up. Why don't I just admit that?"

Gabriel said nothing. He stood there, suit jacket still buttoned, as if he were in a court of law instead of a muddy spring forest.

"I'm making excuses for her again, aren't I?" I said.

"You've never done that, Olivia," he said.

"Yes, I have. I excuse her behavior all the time. God, I can't believe I even still have a relationship with her. After what she did to you? What she did to James?"

"You have a relationship with her because she is your mother. It is not a close relationship, but it is a necessary one. A useful one."

"After everything's she's done—"

"For you."

I growled and spun on him. "That doesn't make it better."

"No, it makes it worse for you. She allowed Tristan to kill James because she thought James was a threat to you. She set me up for his murder because she thought I was a threat to you. I hold her more responsible for his death. What she did to me was a chess move, and I won the match."

"Sending you to prison is not a game, Gabriel."

"It was to her. It was to me. I outwitted her. I proved I am not a threat. I am no longer in danger from her." He stepped toward me. "It doesn't seem as if she did this, Olivia. I know that's not what you want to hear."

"What? I'm the one *accepting* her excuses."

"No, you're the one trying to convince yourself they *are* excuses. It makes no sense for her to set Todd up. She's done everything she can to win his freedom. It also makes no sense for her to follow Ioan to see where the body went, rather than hurry home before Todd realized she was gone. And it makes no sense to put Todd back in prison for another crime. While the law claims that would not affect her own appeal, it most certainly would. She isn't guilty of this, as much as you might wish she was."

I bristled. "I certainly do *not* wish—"

"You mentioned excuses. This is the one you *do* want. The excuse to cut off contact forever. If she did this, you could justify it."

"I should already be able to justify it. After what she's done, I don't need a reason. I don't do it because I lack the damned spine. You cut Seanna from your life. So why can't I do the same with Pamela?"

His voice lowered. "I did that for myself, Olivia. Not to hurt Seanna. Not even because she deserved it. In her current mental state, she might not deserve it, but I can't be sure of that. Regardless of whether she has changed, my experiences of what she did—the reality of what she did—hasn't, so I cannot, for my own sake, rebuild a relationship we never had in the first place. Our situation is different. Your mother, for all her faults, loves you. What she has done may have hurt you, but unlike Seanna, that was not her intention."

I went still as my gut twisted. "God, that was...that was a shitty, shitty comparison to make. I'm *so* sorry."

"You didn't mean it that way, and I did not take it that way. I was simply pointing out—"

"—that I'm comparing the mother who spent twenty years in prison to help me with the one who walked away from you at fifteen, left you to fend for yourself with nothing. The mother who never *gave* you anything in the first place."

"That wasn't what I meant."

"But it's true, and you're right. You're also right that, on some level, I want an excuse. I already have excuses, if I choose to take them. I don't need another. I just need to either accept that I want some form of relationship with Pamela...or decide that I don't. Stop whining about it."

"You don't whine about it, Olivia. No more—I hope—than I did with Seanna. We are conflicted. I'm still not certain I made the right choice. I may change it someday. For now, it feels better than the alternative. For now, what you have with Pamela works. It's a distant and difficult but ultimately useful relationship."

"I know, I'm just…I wish I wouldn't get stuck in these ruts, you know?"

He walked over and took my chin in his hand. Then he kissed me. It started slow but deepened as my anxiety fed into it. He only needed to sense that, and he responded in kind, his arms going around me, pulling me against him. I had his shirt off in record time—well, record time for non-damaging removal. My shirt didn't fare quite so well, which suggested I wasn't the only one stockpiling stress this week. When it tore, he mumbled an apology against my lips, but I silenced it and tore the shirt some more getting it off.

He didn't even attempt the hooks on my bra, just shoved it up. My jeans required far too much work—they might have been a bit snug—so once he popped the button, I took it from there. As for his trousers, well, they didn't need to be *removed*, did they? I got them far enough and nudged him toward the ground, but Gabriel isn't going anywhere he doesn't want to go, and apparently, that wasn't what he had in mind. Instead, he backed into a tree and hoisted me up, and I got the kind of stress relief I'd needed way more than I realized.

Afterward, he held me there, still straddling him as he leaned back against the tree.

I kissed him. "Thank you."

"Thank *you*. I believe I needed that as much as you did."

I glanced at our position. "I should probably let you put me down, as much as I'm loath to suggest it."

"I'm fine. I've been working out."

I laughed and snuggled into him. He leaned back more, getting comfortable while still holding me up.

"Impressive, really," I said.

"Thank you. I will admit that when we met, I wasn't in optimal condition. As my schedule intensified, working out was the first thing to drop off my to-do list. Then, when I decided to woo you away from Ricky, I decided that getting in better shape was necessary if I hoped to compete in that arena. Which was, admittedly, pointless."

"Yeah, I don't exactly compare muscle tone when picking a lover, Gabriel."

"I mean competing in the area of the physical against Ricky is rather like him competing in law against me. And yes, a few extra pounds weren't going to be what kept you from seeing me in a more favorable light. It was simply easier to focus on that rather than do something extreme, like let you *know* I wanted to be with you."

"Uh-huh…"

"However, once we did get together, I realized *that* was the point at which a certain degree of athleticism was required. Possibly also acrobatic training."

I laughed and kissed him one more time before disengaging and sinking to the ground. "I'd love to say that's not necessary, but I feel it wouldn't be in my best interest. Though, if you do ever actually sign up for acrobatics, please tell me. That I'd have to see. And possibly videotape."

He snorted as he pulled up his trousers. "I believe I'll skip the formal training and stick to real-time practice." He reached down for my ripped blouse. "I apologize for this and will replace it… with a shirt that has buttons big enough for my fingers to actually manipulate."

"We'll just start taking all my shirts to the tailor. Get the buttons replaced with snaps."

"Don't joke, or you'll wake up to find all your blouses missing as I take you up on that very reasonable suggestion."

We continued talking as we dressed. Then we headed out. There was nothing to find here, and neither of us commented on that—it'd spoil our good moods. We just started walking, hand in hand, chattering about nonsense and nothing. We'd gone at least a quarter mile before I slowed and looked around.

"Is this the right way?" I asked.

"No, I don't believe it is," Gabriel said, making no move to adjust his direction. "Are we in a hurry?"

"We are not, and this seems a perfectly fine direction to go."

"Agreed."

We continued on, talking in that giddy afterglow way, wandering aimlessly. When I tripped over a branch, Gabriel caught me and pulled me into his arms, and I took advantage of the opportunity for a kiss. Just a quick smack on the lips.

As I pulled back, he grabbed my breast, hard, and I jumped with a gasp because that was *not* like Gabriel. Rough, yes, when that was the direction we took, but not a hard—painfully hard—grab during a casual kiss.

Even as I pulled back, I knew what I'd see. Not Gabriel. And I was right. Shadows swallowed the forest, turning day to night, telling me I'd fallen into a vision.

A figure stood in front of me, at least six inches shorter than Gabriel and nearly that much narrower. He moved toward me, and I went to push him back, but my hands were tied behind me. My heart hammered, panic igniting. The figure moved closer, and my eyes adjusted enough to the darkness for me to see his face.

Gregory Kirkman.

"You like that?" he said, and he reached to grab my breast again. I stumbled backward and tripped as my legs tangled. I crashed to the ground, unable to block my fall with my hands bound. My shoulder hit a rock, and tears of pain sprang to my eyes. My face was already tight with dried tears, my throat hoarse from screaming for help that hadn't come. I opened my mouth to scream again, but a gag stopped me.

As I twisted to get up, Kirkman fell on me.

"In a hurry to get to this part?" he said. "Guess you *did* like it."

The panic exploded. Not just the victim's panic but my own, as I realized what was about to happen. I'd had visions before. Horrible visions of death and loss that gave me nightmares for weeks. Yet I'd been spared this particular nightmare, and now, as Kirkman pinned me to the ground, I went wild with absolute fear. I fought with everything I had, but the girl whose body I inhabited was tiny, and her struggles weren't enough to do more than make him laugh. He lowered his mouth to mine, and I screwed up my focus and tried to burst free from the vision.

Let me out. Please, please, let me out. I can handle anything but this. Please, please, please—

Kirkman's body weight lifted from mine, and I thought my plea had been heard. Instead, he only rose to a crouch, hands still pinning me as he peered into the forest.

I twisted. Through the trees, I could make out a moving figure. Kirkman's hand went to my mouth, as if the gag weren't there. I started making noises through it, grunts and muffled cries, but they were too soft for the other person to hear.

His gaze on the figure, Kirkman slid down to my feet. He took rope from his jacket pocket and tied my ankles together. Then he rose and slipped off to the side, approaching the figure from another direction.

"Hey," he called. "Looking for me?"

"Yeah," a young male voice said. "You weren't at the house, and I know you like coming out here."

"I was just taking a walk. What's up?"

"Uh, Mae's midnight bash? I was picking you up at eleven, right?"

"Shit. Yes. I completely forgot. Better count me out. I worked on the house all day, and I won't make it past midnight."

"You sure?"

"Yeah, sorry. Come by tomorrow, and we'll hang out."

"Sure. I'll give you a shout in the morning."

As they talked, I struggled against my bonds. I grunted and screamed into the gag. I kicked and flailed my bound feet. Once, my legs struck a sapling hard enough to set it shaking, and I was sure whoever Kirkman was speaking to would notice. He didn't. I tried again and set the whole tree quaking, but it gave only the faintest creak. I pushed harder. Leaves rustled as the sapling swayed. It sounded no different than the wind in the trees.

I tried getting to my feet. My shoes slid against the damp ground, unable to find purchase. I flipped over and pulled my legs up, inchworm style and began to rise like that—

"What the hell are you doing?" Kirkman said, sounding more amused than angry as his hand clasped my shirt. He hauled me upright and clamped his fingers over my gag. "Shhh. Shhh. Sorry for the interruption, but he's leaving."

Sure enough, footsteps receded down the path. When they were gone, Kirkman whispered in my ear. Whispered things that made me fight and scream against the gag. He stepped back. Smiled. Kicked my bound legs. I went down face-first. He straddled my back and put his hands around my neck.

As his fingers tightened, my head shot up, eyes bulging. I saw something in the forest. A flash of movement. Then a figure appeared, slinking through the trees, hunched over. He stopped, almost on eye level with me, less than twenty feet away.

I saw his face. And he saw me. He looked straight at me. I screamed against my gag, a gurgling scream as Kirkman choked me.

Help me. Please. I know you can see me. Please, please, please.

The world grayed at the edges as I lost consciousness. And the last thing I saw was that face in the forest. Watching me. Just watching.

~⁓

I snapped from the vision with a start. Gabriel was on the ground, holding me, his hand against my fevered forehead.

"It's okay," he murmured. "It's okay."

When he saw my eyes open, he exhaled in relief and shifted as he checked my eyes, rechecked my forehead, making sure my rising temperature hadn't exploded into a full-blown fever. Then he asked, "Did you—?" He stopped. Saw my face and said, "You did."

I tried to answer but could only nod, my teeth chattering. He pulled me closer and rubbed down the goosebumps on my arm.

"Do you want to talk about it?" he asked.

"I will," I managed to croak. "Just…" I shivered. "I need a moment."

"Of course," he said, and his arms tightened around me as I curled up against him, sitting on the forest floor and trying desperately not to think about what had happened here, all those years ago.

EIGHTEEN

GABRIEL

OLIVIA DID eventually tell him what happened. She tried to start at the end, with seeing the person in the forest, but she struggled to stay there, and he'd asked her to go back. To tell the whole thing. As soon as she did, he wished he hadn't.

He did not wish he hadn't heard it. He wished he hadn't asked. When he realized what she was saying, he wished he hadn't agreed to come here at all.

What the hell had he been thinking?

That wasn't entirely fair. He knew what they'd both been thinking—that if Olivia had a vision, it would return her to the killing of Gregory Kirkman. While he'd argued against that, she'd insisted, and he'd had to admit that, since she'd seen it once, it was already in her head. She wouldn't be focusing on Kirkman's murder anyway—she'd be trying to glean more information about the person in the woods.

They had not considered the possibility that she'd witness one of the murders…from inside the victim. It made sense, though. Olivia had seen Todd and Kirkman through Todd's memories. Coming back to that spot might not spark a vision of that memory. However, one of the victims—Laura Simmons, the girl from Cainsville—had fae blood. Hers was the story this place wanted to tell. Hers was the one Olivia's fae blood would show her. The rape and murder of a teenage girl from Cainsville. If Gabriel had even considered that, he'd have done everything in his power to keep Olivia away from this spot even if it'd meant making her angry enough to kick him out of the house.

His own nightmares of *that* scenario—Olivia throwing him out—seemed laughable compared to what she could have suffered here. He just hadn't thought—no, he hadn't *thought*. Full stop. He should have, and he had not. He could only be thankful now that the vision had set her free when the girl lost consciousness.

Once Olivia retold the early part of the vision, she could focus on the rest. On the man in the forest. He'd sounded young, she said. Not a child but younger than Kirkman. He'd come to take Kirkman to a midnight party given by someone named Mae. Considering that Kirkman was known to be a loner, this struck both of them as unusual. Yet Kirkman had seemed to know the young man well, and the young man knew *him* well enough to suspect he was in the forest. Then the young man had watched. He'd pretended to leave, snuck back and watched what Kirkman did to his victim.

Gabriel had some idea who the young man might have been. Not specifically who he was, but who he might be in relation to Kirkman. He filed that in the back of his mind without telling Olivia his suspicions. Let her research it without bias.

Research was indeed the next step. Olivia was already on her cell phone browser as they walked out of the forest. When Gabriel's own phone rang, the noise startled her.

"Detective Parsons," Gabriel said, and then answered.

His first thought was that someone from the police department had spotted his car near the crime scene. He answered the call with his explanation ready. Instead, Detective Parsons was phoning to let him know that they no longer considered Todd a viable suspect. The social security card had been real, but when an expert examined the business card, they determined it'd been printed recently and artificially weathered before being placed in Kirkman's pocket. Which suggested the body had been disturbed. The police had already considered that. The state of the burial had suggested it. They would conduct further tests on the body to see whether the soil on it matched the soil where he'd been found. If not, that suggested the body had been moved closer to the girl's corpse in anticipation of framing Todd.

"I have no idea what's going on here," Detective Parsons said. "But I thought I should let you know we're not actively pursuing Todd as a suspect at this time. I'm sure Olivia will be glad to hear that."

"She will. Thank you."

The detective paused. "There's something else."

Gabriel knew there was. Detective Parsons was a considerate person, who would realize how worried Olivia was over this. She was also interested—for her own purposes—in maintaining a good relationship with Gabriel. However, neither of those things meant she'd call just to tell Gabriel they weren't pursuing Todd as an active suspect.

"We heard from our anonymous informant again," she said. "Unfortunately, the operator didn't realize that we considered this a person of interest. He did, however, know that we weren't actively pursuing Todd Larsen."

"And told this to the caller."

"No, he wouldn't make that mistake. The caller was very interested in the status of the case. He identified himself as the earlier informant and wanted to know why Todd Larsen was still walking around when we'd found Gregory Kirkman's body. The operator assured him we were investigating all possibilities, which was enough, apparently, for the caller to realize we wouldn't be arresting Todd anytime soon. He became extremely upset, enough so that the operator realized something was suspicious. The caller hung up before a trace could be initiated."

Detective Parsons exhaled. "I thought you should know. I don't like the sound of that call, particularly in conjunction with your theory from earlier. We're pursuing this angle, but you should keep an eye on Todd. You might want to notify the local police and get a protective detail on him. If they can't do it, I'll see if there's any chance of us covering it from the state side."

Gabriel thanked her again. When he hung up, Olivia still had her attention glued to her phone. His side of the conversation hadn't been enough to alarm her, so she'd gone back to her research.

"Olivia?" he said.

She held up her phone. On the screen was an old photograph of a man in his mid-twenties. "Meet Barry Kirkman."

"Gregory's brother?"

"Yep. Greg was the oldest of three. Barry is the youngest. In the middle is Mae, who was having that midnight party."

Gabriel nodded. This was what he'd suspected. A loner known to avoid socializing might still maintain close ties with his family. Gabriel knew that from experience. A younger man who knew him well? One who seemed to share his proclivities? That suggested a brother.

"Which doesn't mean Barry *must* have been the guy in the forest the night Kirkman died," Olivia continued. "He's a very strong suspect, though. He sees my father kill his brother. He's too afraid to intercede—and it happened very, very fast. Then he keeps watching and sees where Ioan put the body. He might have been deciding how to handle it when my father was arrested. Coming forward then meant Todd would tell the world that Greg was a serial killer. My father went to prison, and that was good enough for Barry... until Todd got out. Now it's too late to positively pin any crimes on Greg, so it can be slanted to seem as if Greg found Todd with Laura Simmons's body and got killed for it. Greg's a hero. Todd's a killer. Barry gets his revenge. I'll find out more about Barry tonight, and we can pay him a visit in the morning."

"We may want to do that now," Gabriel said, and he told her about Detective Parsons's concerns.

NINETEEN

OLIVIA

I HAD an address for Barry Kirkman before we got to the car. According to my research, Barry was married with two kids—a college-aged son and a teenage daughter—and he lived in a suburb between Cainsville and Chicago. Twenty minutes after leaving the forest, we were outside Barry's house.

We'd parked a block over and walked. Kirkman's house was on a corner lot with only a chainlink fence, and we'd stopped there, as if talking, while I got a better look at the place. The dining room was at the back, and I could see Barry setting the table as a woman put out dinner. A daughter joined, and they all sat. Their heads bowed in grace, and my teeth gritted at that as I remembered Barry Kirkman's face watching his brother strangle Laura Simmons. Watching and doing nothing to help her. Watching and enjoying.

On the way here, I'd called Ricky and asked him to keep Todd inside for a while. They'd just been heading out, it seemed. Now I called back to say it was fine to go. We had eyes on Barry Kirkman, and he was otherwise occupied. We'd keep watch for a while and figure out a way to speak to him.

TWENTY

RICKY

TODD HAD just about had enough of this whole babysitting business. Ricky didn't blame him. He didn't blame Liv, either, for insisting on it. Her dad just got out of jail, and now he was under threat. Of course she'd want a twenty-four-hour watch on him. But the fact Todd had spent those twenty years in prison meant that he was accustomed to looking out for himself, and he didn't appreciate being treated like a defenseless target.

Ricky got that, better than Liv or Gabriel could. He'd known guys who'd done time, and as laid-back as Todd might seem, the babysitting rankled. Ricky joked about it being bodyguard duty instead, but that didn't make it much better. Either way, it said Todd needed protection, and a kid half his age had been assigned to provide it.

Speaking of kids…

A guy had been following them. He wasn't much younger than Ricky. At first, Ricky figured *he* was the one who'd sparked the kid's interest. The guy had been checking out Ricky's jacket, and then he'd taken out his phone, his gaze moving between that and the jacket, as if searching for the logo online.

Ricky had first noticed the kid on Main Street. He'd followed them to the hardware store. That's where Todd had wanted to go earlier, before Liv called and put them on lockdown. Todd knew Liv wanted an addition to their house, and he was planning one for her as a gift, but also, Ricky suspected, as a project. Something to sharpen his skills before he resumed his carpentry work. That was Todd's plan—getting back into his old business.

The question was whether anyone would want to hire exonerated serial killer, Todd Larsen. Even those who agreed he was innocent might not want him in their houses. Todd knew that. He was under no illusions that "acquitted" meant "innocent" to everyone or even to most people. He had a plan for dealing with that, which he'd discussed with Ricky, who knew plenty of guys who'd had to rebuild their own rep after a prison stint or after leaving a gang.

Ricky and Todd also had another plan, one that Liv was going to like a helluva lot less than the career rehabilitation. But, well, Todd was a grown man, forty-six years old and eager to put his life back on track. That would mean moving faster toward an independent life than his daughter might like. Liv would not appreciate Ricky's "intervention" in this right away, but she'd be fine with it once she realized Todd wouldn't melt into the ozone if she stopped watching over him.

As for the guy following them, it was only as they neared the hardware store that Ricky realized Todd was his target. Ricky had caught him taking a few photos, and he could tell by the angle that *he* wasn't the main subject.

Liv really wasn't going to like that. The kid must be a local—Cainsville didn't exactly attract outsiders that age. So this local kid had heard that Todd Larsen was in town, and he'd set out to snap a few pics for Instagram. Even better, he now had photos of Todd accompanied by a biker. Someone seeing those shots would eventually identify Ricky as Liv's ex, so he wasn't too worried about the "biker" connection hurting Todd, but it'd still be the kind of press Liv would rather avoid. Which meant Ricky had to do something about it. The fact this kid was a local meant Ricky couldn't pull a Gabriel and snatch the phone away. It had to be handled more delicately.

Ricky accompanied Todd into the hardware shop. As he did, he caught a glimpse of... He wasn't sure what he saw. A shimmer of motion behind them, the door staying open a fraction too long after they entered.

Fae. He knew that instinctively. Liv had caught a curious fae following him and Todd yesterday, and it seemed that fae hadn't learned her lesson.

Ricky looked around the store. It was empty except for Gordon Webster—the doc's brother and store owner—stocking shelves. Safe enough especially at midday. He'd tell Gabriel to have another chat with the elders. For now...

"I'm going to wait outside," Ricky said.

Todd seemed relieved. A few minutes free of his shadow. Todd said he was going to speak to Webster, and Ricky stepped back out the front door. The kid had ducked around the side, doing nearly as lousy a job of hiding as that damned fae.

Ricky checked his phone. He'd surreptitiously snapped shots of the kid as they'd walked. Most were useless—the subject barely in the frame—but he found a decent one and zoomed in on the guy's face. Then he went into his contacts, dug up Patrick's number and sent it to him with a note.

Two minutes later, a response came.

Patrick: *Not local.*

Ricky: *You sure?*

Patrick: *Yep. Not many kids that age in town.*

Damn. He wanted Patrick to say, *Oh yes, that was so-and-so's son,* and they'd go have a chat with him and sort this out. They'd use their fae powers of compulsion to convince the guy not to post those pictures, and everything would be fine.

Ricky glanced into the hardware store. Todd was talking to Webster. There was no sign of the fae. Ricky didn't like walking away and leaving Todd with her but… Well, this was Cainsville. There were plenty of fae, all curious by nature, and with the extra precautions the elders had taken for Todd's return, Ricky couldn't imagine a random malicious one wandering around undetected. Even if that were the case, it was only six p.m. and Todd was talking to a human. He'd be safe, and Ricky didn't expect this to take long.

Ricky took one last look at Todd. Then he headed toward the intruder still hiding beside the shop. As Ricky approached, he studied the guy's shadow extending out onto the sidewalk. He seemed to be doing something. Fussing with his phone? Uploading those pictures? Shit.

Ricky picked up speed. An alley ran between the hardware store and the neighboring shop. A typical Cainsville alley—a bright, manicured walkway, rather than a dark, urban invitation to a mugging. It'd still be useful, though, secluded as it was. Ricky could confront the guy in there and—

He stopped. The building beside the hardware store had a side window. It was blocked on the inside, probably because it overlooked a solid wall. The glass reflected the guy in the alley. It showed what he held in his hand…and it wasn't a cell phone.

It was a gun.

Ricky paused just long enough to be absolutely sure he wasn't misidentifying a bottle or a knife or anything else. He wasn't. He might not carry a gun himself, but the Saints made most of their profit from the sale of ones just like this.

Ricky took another second to consider the possibility of apprehending the kid without getting shot. Yeah, no, he wasn't ever going to be that stupid. Even if he snuck around the building, he risked being heard the second he stepped into the alley. A kid like that could be spooked into pulling the trigger.

Ricky retreated slowly. Then he hurried into the hardware shop and jogged to Todd.

"We need to go," he said.

Todd raised a "just a minute" finger.

"No, now." Ricky clasped Todd's elbow. That startled Webster, and Todd balked, but Ricky propelled him out the back door.

"I just needed another minute," Todd said, voice sharp with irritation. "Whatever Liv is worried about, it could have waited—"

"Guy," Ricky said as he kept Todd moving. "Gun."

"What?" Todd wrenched from Ricky's grasp.

"A kid was following us. He has a gun. I don't. We need to get back—"

Todd didn't need Ricky to finish. He broke into a jog. Ricky took off after him and—

Something hit him. That's all he knew. Something slammed into his side and knocked him clean off his feet. Cold fingers clamped around his throat even as he sailed through the air.

He fumbled to grab for the hands, and he felt an arm, an ice-cold, rock-solid arm. Fingers dug into the side of his neck…and everything went dark.

TWENTY-ONE

OLIVIA

BARRY KIRKMAN was walking his dog. He'd left the house after dinner, leading a dog that Lloergan could swallow in a mouthful. Hell, TC was bigger than this canine. I didn't know the breed, but it had short and stubby legs that tired easily, and before Barry had gone a quarter mile, he was carrying the pooch. He didn't head back, though. He kept walking, as if this excursion was more about him than the dog. That made me think he had a goal in mind, that "I'm walking the dog" was just an excuse. Yet we'd been following him since he started, and he'd stayed within the neighborhood, nothing here except houses. He hadn't even taken out his phone. Nor had he checked his watch as if he needed to meet someone. He just walked.

Once I was sure nothing interesting was about to happen, I made it happen. I skirted down a side street, and when Barry turned the next corner, I was there, pretending to open a community mailbox. He started walking past, and I turned right in his path. And there I was, staring into the middle-aged face of the young man I'd seen in the forest. The one who'd watched Greg Kirkman strangle Laura Simmons.

Barry looked at me. There was a split second of trying to place me within this environment. I looked familiar, and I was in his sub-division, at the mailbox, therefore I must be a neighbor. That lasted only long enough for him to take a better look. Then, with a flash of recognition, he finally placed me. Dismay, fear, and apprehension flickered over his face.

"Hello, Barry," I said.

He glanced over his shoulder, presumably considering a fast retreat. Gabriel stood a half-dozen steps away. Barry's arms tightened around his dog, who wriggled in annoyance.

"I want to talk to you about some calls you've been making," I said.

A look crossed his face, feigned confusion. "Calls?"

"About my father."

"Calls about your father?" That look of confusion again. Then it vanished with a slight widening of his eyes, as if he'd missed a cue. His eyes shuttered. "I'm afraid I don't know who you mean. Does your dad live around here?"

I said nothing. He looked back at Gabriel, who was now on his phone, appearing to have stopped paying attention, but Barry knew better than to test that. When he looked back at me, his Adam's apple bobbed.

"You'll need to tell me who your father is, miss," he said. "We've only lived here a year and…"

He trailed off as he saw the look on my own face. The one that said I wasn't falling for this, wasn't playing along.

"Your brother," I said, and that was all it took. He couldn't hold in his emotions then. His face practically exploded with them— hate, rage and then, fear.

After a moment, he collected himself and said, "I don't know what this is about, but I really must be going."

"Must you?" I said as he turned. "That's odd. Your brother has been missing for twenty-five years. His body has just been discovered. Now a stranger shows up talking about him, and you turn away? One would think you'd be eager for information, for clues as to how he died. Turning away like that..." I purse my lips. "It's almost as if you already know."

Now he pivoted slowly back to me. "What is that supposed to mean?"

"Someone placed an anonymous call to the police, leading them to your brother's body."

"What?"

"You seem surprised. Weird, when it was right there, in the news."

"I haven't read the news. I don't want to see what they have to say."

"About Greg? Why not? He didn't do anything wrong, did he?"

Barry flinched.

I continued. "The reason I'm here is that someone is connecting your murdered brother to my father. Someone planted a fake business card in Greg's pocket, one supposedly belonging to Todd Larsen...only it was printed just a few weeks ago."

Emotions fluttered, too fast for me to catch. "I-I don't know—"

"Laura Simmons," I said.

"Wh-what?" He choked the word out, and there was no confusion on his face now, no lack of recognition. With that name, his face drained of blood, and he could barely stammer out the question.

I stepped toward him and lowered my voice. "You watched your brother strangle her. She begged you for help. *Begged.* And you watched. You enjoyed watching."

He couldn't even form words, mouth opening and closing as he tried. Sweat trickled down his brow, and his dog whimpered as he clutched it tight.

"I-I don't know what—" he managed, his voice squeaking.

"You watched. You liked watching. You sick son-of-a-bitch."

"No. *No.*" He was shaking now. "I don't know who told you—"

"No one needed to tell me." I leaned forward and whispered details. Where it happened. What he'd been wearing. What his brother did. Barry didn't ask how I knew. He was too panicked to think of that.

"I've changed," he said. "I never—I never did anything. Never hurt anyone. Whatever sickness I had, it's cured. I found God, and he saved me, and I'm a different man now. A good man."

"A good man?" I laughed. "A good man would have gone to the police and told them the truth. A good man would have given those families closure. A good man would have let his brother go down in history as a killer. That's justice. That's righteousness. Your God doesn't exist to shield you from your shitty choices, Barry. Don't hide behind him. I'm sure he doesn't appreciate it."

Barry Kirkman just kept gibbering excuses and insistences that he was a good man, that he'd changed, that he'd never actually done anything.

"Right," I said. "You didn't *do* anything. You watched your brother murder a girl, and then you kept his secret so he could do it again. When he ended up dead, you found his body, and you decided to plant my father's business card on it. You knew they'd worked together, and you're such a damned coward that you wanted my father in prison for your brother's crimes, so there was no chance your family name would be tarnished. No chance anyone would ever take a closer look at *you.*"

I'd reworked the story this way, framing it to avoid anything actually connecting my father to Kirkman's death. Of course, if Barry had been there, he knew who killed his brother. But he only mewled weak denials.

"You knew where to find your brother's body."

"Yes, but I didn't tell—"

"You knew where to find his body," I said.

"I saw…" He ran one hand through his thinning hair. "I-I don't even know what I saw that night. I was staying with Greg. He'd been out, and I heard him come home and go straight into the forest. I followed and…"

He looked at me. He could say he saw Todd murder Greg, but he seemed to realize that might not be the right move here.

"I…I don't even know what I saw. I just wanted it to go away. Whatever happened, whatever my brother did, it's over."

"Someone called the police two days ago to report your brother's body and link it to my father."

"It wasn't me. I was at a retreat. No phones. No electronics. I needed a few days of peace when…" *When your father got out.* That's what he meant. Instead, he said, "I needed peace."

"Who did you tell about your brother's burial place?"

"No one. I wouldn't…"

He trailed off, and his eyes widened.

"You told someone," I said. "Tell me who it was."

TWENTY-TWO

OLIVIA

I COULDN'T get Ricky or my father on the phone. There were others I could have called in Cainsville. I didn't. Gabriel drove as fast as he could, and I kept speed-dialing Ricky and Todd, telling myself it was fine; they were probably out back with a beer and had left their phones inside. Except Ricky never left his phone anywhere. Ever.

The alternative, though, was that they were unable to call because someone was in Cainsville. A young man who wanted my father to pay for killing his uncle.

Matthew Kirkman. Barry's twenty-year-old son. That was who he'd told four years ago in a drunken rant. It seemed that while Barry had found religion, he hadn't managed to locate sobriety. On what would have been his brother's birthday, he'd gotten loaded on a fishing trip with Matt and told him the whole story. Well, told him a variation of it.

In this version, good old Uncle Greg had tried to stop that maniac, Todd Larsen, from killing a young woman. Before Barry could intervene, Todd murdered Greg. While burying Greg a few miles away, Todd caught Barry watching and warned that if he told anyone, he'd kill his entire family. Does this make any sense? Of course not. Later, when Barry sobered up and Matt confronted him, he had the sense to backpedal. It wasn't true—just a nightmare he'd had once, and it came back when he drank. He'd thought Matt accepted the nightmare excuse. Obviously not.

I could notify Patrick or one of the other elders, but what we were dealing with here was more dangerous than any fae. It was a very angry young man, one who had been gifted a handgun when he went off to college in Chicago.

We left Barry assuring us that his son wasn't a threat and that he'd speak to him. We didn't push further, so he took that to mean we'd leave the matter in his hands. Then we found Matt's cell phone number online. That's surprisingly easy to do with a twenty-year-old college student. We called and got voice mail, which assured us this was "Matt" and he'd call back as soon as he finished whatever he was doing.

We found out soon enough what he was doing. Exactly what I'd feared. The whole way home, I'd kept telling myself I was being paranoid. What were the chances that Matt Kirkman would strike against my father now? Just as we uncovered the identity of our threat? Pretty good, it seemed.

Like Detective Parsons said, Matt was pissed. The police weren't moving, and when you're twenty years old, and you have a gun, you don't sit around hoping the cops change their mind.

Matt was in the parlor with Todd. I could see figures through the side window, and that window was cracked open enough for us to catch voices. I couldn't make out what Matt was saying.

Where was Ricky? Presumably there, either incapacitated or keeping quiet. When I moved, I thought I saw a third figure on the sofa. That must be Ricky.

Gabriel motioned for me to go around and see whether the back door was open. He'd take the front.

I eased open the rear gate and jogged through and onto the back deck, where a couple of nearly empty beers said Dad and Ricky had been out here at some point. They'd failed to secure the patio door. Well, they'd locked it, but they hadn't braced the sliding glass door, which meant my key opened it.

Through the kitchen door, I could see the security panel, all blinking green. I slipped inside.

Voices drifted out. Matt was telling his father's side of the story. When he paused for breath, Todd said, "Does that make sense?" and I winced.

Don't, Dad. Don't question him. Just hold on, and keep him talking.

I adjusted my grip on my gun. Through the front door window, Gabriel spotted me. He motioned that he'd come around the back. I continued creeping toward the parlor.

"What?" Matt said.

"Does it make any sense?" Todd said, his voice soothing, calm. "Can you really see your father hiding while he watched me kill his brother?"

"He was young. He was scared."

"He was about your age, right? Would you have hid?"

"I—"

"So, he hid and then calmly followed to see where I buried your uncle? How many times would he have had the opportunity to sneak up and take me down? Or to see that I'd be stuck a while, digging a grave, and run to call the police?"

No, Dad. Please. Just stop.

"Are you suggesting my father lied to me?" Matt said.

"Yes, I'm sorry, son, but I am. I'm suggesting I wasn't the one who murdered that girl."

I clenched my teeth. What the hell was my father doing? I took another two steps along the front hall. Then I stopped. Through the parlor doorway, I could see Matt's arm. I could see the gun. I could tell he was facing my way, and as soon as I took another step, he'd spot me.

I turned around as Gabriel stepped inside. I quickly motioned for him to return to the front door.

Todd—damn him—was still talking. "I'm going to suggest, son, that the real killer was your uncle."

"What the hell?" Matt's voice rose. "Are you accusing my father—?"

"—of killing your uncle, yes."

"What the hell?" It came out shrill now.

Was Dad trying to *provoke* the kid into shooting him? If so, he was doing an excellent job of it.

I aimed my own weapon, ready to step forward.

Todd continued. "I believe the version that makes sense is a true tragedy, one I played no part in. Your father stumbled over your uncle with that girl. She wasn't the first body found in those woods, or so the police tell me. Your dad found your uncle, and he tried to save the girl, and in doing that, he killed your uncle. He failed to save that poor girl, but he did stop your father. He's a hero."

"Then why the hell wouldn't he just say that?"

"Because he killed his own brother. The sin of Cain, isn't it? You said your father has become religious, and if I recall my Bible right, that's right there. Fratricide. The first murder ever committed. Of course, in this case, your father did the right thing, trying to save that girl. But if he comes forward, he has to admit he killed his brother. He also has to admit his brother was a serial killer. Wouldn't it be better if another serial killer was responsible for all those deaths? One who was in prison for life already? He must have heard your uncle mention my name—we worked on a job together—and when I was arrested, your dad had the perfect scapegoat if anyone found your uncle's body. He'd worked it out to the point where maybe he even believed it himself."

"I…" Matt trailed off, and that gun lowered, dropping to his side as if he didn't realize he was lowering it.

"Doesn't that fit your father better? The hero forced to kill his own brother to save others? So racked with guilt over that biblical crime that he blames a convicted serial killer instead?"

"I…"

Todd continued, his already soothing voice taking on a hypnotic note. "I'm afraid your uncle wasn't a good man. I knew that when I met him. Maybe I should have said something. I didn't. Your father is the one who stopped him, and now he's been forced to live with that for twenty-five years."

Silence from Matt, but that gun stayed at his side, hanging from his hand.

"I didn't kill those girls," Todd said. "When the police came to me yesterday, my lawyer looked up his notes. We have very, very good notes on my whereabouts leading up to my alleged crimes. At the time that girl disappeared, I was in Wisconsin with my wife and daughter on a weeklong job. I did not kill her, just like I didn't kill those four couples."

Movement. I tensed, but it was just Todd stepping forward to take the gun from Matt, who let him have it.

"Let's sit down and talk," Todd said.

AS much as I wanted to run in there and resolve this, I knew Todd had it under control. Having Gabriel and me join would only spook the kid. Still, I did call after I'd slipped back outside. Todd's cell phone rang from just inside the back door, and when he came to answer it, he saw me, told Matt that he had to take the call and then came outside, watching through the kitchen doorway in case the kid bolted.

"I heard everything," I said. "We were coming to rescue you but…"

"I didn't need it?" Todd said with a smile.

"Yeah, sorry."

He handed me Matt's gun. "I'll let you take this. I think he'll be fine—I've talked him down. But I was just about to take a break and call you. You need to find Ricky."

My gut seized. "He's not with you?"

Todd shook his head, and Gabriel stepped up behind me as I said, "What happened?"

"Something fae," Todd said. "Ricky saw the kid, knew he was following us and spotted the gun. He hustled me out of the hardware store. We were making tracks back here. I was in front. I heard something. I looked back and…I'm not even sure what I saw. Something had him."

"Some*thing?*" My voice went tight.

"Someone," he corrected quickly. "A fae. I only caught a blur. Ricky was in the air and—"

"The *air?*"

Gabriel's hand gripped my shoulder, reassurance but also a warning to let my father finish.

"It happened fast," Todd said. "A fae had him. I took off after them, but they disappeared. I'd left my phone here, so I ran to get it and call you, and I forgot about the kid. He caught up. I'm sure Ricky's fine. It's Cainsville. There are fae, and one just made a mistake."

"We'll find him," Gabriel said.

TWENTY-THREE

OLIVIA

I RAN for Veronica's house. The wards had obviously been broken, and there was no harm in waking her. I'd reached the next corner before I realized driving would have been faster. Gabriel's car pulled up beside me.

I hopped in.

"Veronica?" he said.

As I nodded, my phone buzzed with a text. I fumbled with it, hoping for Ricky or even for Todd telling me he remembered something else. Instead, it was Patrick, and I would have put the phone down again if I hadn't seen Ricky's name in that first line of the text.

I opened the text and skimmed it. It seemed Ricky had sent Patrick a photo of a young man, asking if he was local. Patrick had said the boy wasn't local, and he'd texted for more, to satisfy his curiosity, but Ricky hadn't answered. So he was trying me.

I called. Patrick answered on the first ring.

"What are you kids up to this—?" he began.

"Cainsville," I said. "Flying fae."

When he didn't answer fast enough, I said, "Patrick. Flying fae in Cainsville. What do you know?"

"Flying…? Fae don't fly, Liv. I would make a joke about Tinkerbell wings, but I can tell by your voice that this is not the—"

"It isn't. A fae attacked Ricky behind the hardware store. It flew off with him."

"*Flew* off?" Silence. Then, he swore, "*Cach*."

"Patrick…"

"Damn, Grace. I told her—"

"I don't care about Grace right now. What took Ricky?"

He exhaled. "You're in the car, yes? I hear the motor. Are you in Cainsville?"

"Heading to speak to Veronica."

"Turn onto Walnut. Take Peach to the end. There's an abandoned house there."

"At the end of Peach? Bullshit, Patrick. I jog that way all the time. It's a dead end. There's nothing—"

"Just go there. Park and wait for me. Don't go any farther. *Wait for me*. Understand?"

I made a noise of assent and hung up.

ALL roads in Cainsville ended within Cainsville—except Main, which became the regional highway leading out. It was an odd construction quirk that you didn't notice until you stopped to think about it. After all, if you wanted to leave town, you'd use Main. No reason to go another way. Except you literally could not go another way. Each street ended in a polite Dead End sign, most stopping at the last house, but a few, like Peach, extending beyond the residential area to branch off in fields and forests for hikes and jogs and dog-walks. You had Cainsville, the town, and then you had nothing for a mile or so in each direction before more roads and farms started.

Gabriel pulled in at the end of Peach, right in front of the Dead End sign.

"There's no house here," I said. "It's a stalling tactic. While we stand around, waiting, Patrick will find Ricky. Then we'll get a call—*Oh, did I say Peach? I meant Pansy. By the way, Ricky's turned up, and he's just fine.*"

I paced as I seethed. While I ranted, I kept up an internal loop of "Ricky's fine. He's just fine." It was Cainsville. No fae could swoop in and take him. Why would they? It'd cause too much trouble. A fae had grabbed him by mistake or maybe because, hell, maybe because he was cute, and she was lonely.

I still worried. I paced, and I snarled, and I snapped, and I worried. Gabriel prowled about, looking for a drive or a path.

"There's nothing here," I said. "It's a dead end. I've been here many times, Gabriel. We both have. There's nothing—"

He disappeared. One second he was there, and then he stepped into the forest and disappeared altogether, as if the shadows had swallowed him whole.

"Gabriel?"

When he didn't reply, I hurried into the forest after him, and he stepped from behind a tree, like it had hidden him from view. It hadn't—it was barely more than a sapling. An optical illusion of sorts, and if I hadn't been paying attention, I might indeed have thought I simply lost sight of him as he passed behind trees.

His brows arched as I jogged over.

"You didn't hear me?" I asked.

His expression told me he hadn't.

"Could you see me?" I said.

Another arch of his brows. I explained, and he admitted he hadn't looked my way. I experimented, proving that there was fae magic here, a barrier of sorts. Which might mean Patrick wasn't actually lying...

It only took a few more steps to see that he wasn't. A few steps to reach an overgrown driveway leading to an old farmhouse. From the road, both the house and the drive were invisible. Yet if you happened, for some inexplicable reason, to tramp through that strip of forest—rather than take one of the welcoming, groomed trails farther down—you'd come across this house, and it would seem as if it had only been hidden behind the trees. This was how most fae magic worked. Humans weren't even aware they were seeing anything magical. Their minds filled in the question marks with plausible explanations.

We circled the house, staying in the trees. It looked abandoned, which to me screamed "fae." They loved abandoned places, with a delicious glee. Human expansion drove fae to the New World, and its continued expansion there meant the fae had fewer and fewer wild refuges, the elements increasingly tainted by pollution. When a place was abandoned, nature reclaimed it, and the fae returned, delighting in these small triumphs of Mother Nature over human civilization.

The house was a perfect example of that. It'd nearly been swallowed by greenery, paint and windows long gone, leaving weathered and mossy wood. Stonework crumbled. Iron railings rusted and fell away. A gorgeous ruin, and my fae blood quickened at the sight.

Gabriel chose a window in the back where the forest had crept almost to the building itself. An easy and discreet entry point.

"Patrick said we should wait for him," I whispered.

For the third time, I got that wordless arch of his brows.

"I'm not saying we *should*," I said. "I'm just pointing it out. Covering my ass."

He snorted a soft laugh and shed his jacket and tie, hanging them on a broken branch as if it were a convenient coat hook. Then he eyed the window.

"I'll go first," I said. "And I won't watch you struggle to get through."

"I was simply—"

"Yeah, yeah."

I climbed onto the window frame. The glass had been gone so long there weren't even stray shards to worry about, the wood as smooth and soft as driftwood. I hopped down and, as promised, kept my back turned while Gabriel came through. No amount of exercise was going to let a guy his size gracefully vault through a window frame.

By the time he got in, I was already across the empty room. It was still early evening outside, but in here, I might need a flashlight. I stepped through a doorway, considering the lighting, when out of the corner of my eye, a figure loomed. I spun, gun rising to see...

A gargoyle.

It was a big one, nearly as tall as me, and it was indeed looming, clawed hands outstretched to grab unwary guests.

Interesting choice of hallway decoration.

I touched the stone. Cold. I don't know what else I was expecting. Still, as I continued into the next room, I couldn't help keeping an eye on the statue, as if it might glide after me. I also couldn't help watching for Gabriel's reaction as he stepped into the hall. I could warn him, but that'd be no fun at all.

And, as I should have expected, "no fun at all" was exactly what I got. Gabriel walked into the hall, glanced at the gargoyle and gave it a cursory once-over without even a blink of surprise.

I continued into the next room and found more gargoyles. At least a half dozen. The ones in town were classic gargoyles and grotesques and chimeras. These looked more fae. Twisted and wizened fae.

"An early batch?" I whispered to Gabriel.

He knelt to examine one. The stonework did indeed look older than the ones in town. Cracked and dusty and discolored and moss-freckled. Like the statues in my back garden before I began restoring them.

It would make sense if these did represent early efforts. The Tylwyth Teg may have initially modeled their stone guardians after fae, and later decided they'd be less noticeable if they resembled standard gargoyles.

A floorboard creaked overhead. I looked across the room to see stairs through the doorway. I went up, gun in hand. From the top, I could see open doors and more gargoyles through them. I headed for the room overtop the one downstairs where we'd heard the noise. Through the open doorway, I could see there was no one inside. Just more gargoyles. Three of them in what had once been a bedroom, now empty except for those statues.

I walked to one that looked more like the style in town, a true gargoyle, dog sized and crouched, with fangs and a snout, batwings wrapped around itself. As I touched those wings, I remembered what my father had said.

Something had grabbed Ricky and flown off with him.

A noise again, still overhead.

The attic.

When I slipped into the hall, Gabriel was already opening the only closed door. Beyond it lay more stairs. He motioned for me to take the lead if I wanted. I crept over and then ascended, trying not to sneeze as each step sent up a flurry of dust. Light shone through the broken windows, and an eddy of wind set more dust flying.

As soon as I reached the top, I saw Ricky. He lay on the floor, unconscious, his chest rising with steady breaths. In front of him crouched a gargoyle. It was the size of a child, gray stone carved into a forbidding face. I'd seen it before in town. It came and went more often than the others with no discernible pattern.

As I took a step, the stone figure shimmered. Another step. The gargoyle seemed to pulse and expand. Another, and then it wasn't a gargoyle at all, but an old woman. No, an old *fae*, one who looked the age the elders pretended to be, which made her the oldest I'd ever seen. Even the senior fae in Grace's apartment building looked only middle-aged to me. This one had long iron-gray hair and a deeply creased face.

She stayed crouched, her gaze fixed on Ricky. I took yet another step.

"Mallt-y-Dydd," she said, her voice a whispery creak. Then bright green eyes lasered me. "Or is it Mallt-y-Nos?"

"It's both," I said.

She rose, and even with a slight stoop in her shoulders, she towered over me. Her gaze shot to Gabriel, acknowledging him. Then she looked again at me.

"It cannot be both," she said. "You must choose."

"Yeah, I decided not to," I said. "It's this or nothing. If you have a problem with that—"

"I have a problem with him." She waved at Ricky. "Arawn misled you. They all did—all the Cŵn Annwn."

"No." I walked over and knelt beside Ricky, and she didn't try to stop me, just narrowed those bright green eyes. "The Huntsmen have been honest and fair in all their dealings—"

"Child," she spat. "Such a child. You see a pretty and charming boy, and you fall for his lies. I heard him with your father. Wooing him away from you. Securing him for the Cŵn Annwn."

I sighed. "Whatever you heard—"

"The boy offered your father a place to live," she said. "He suggested your father move out of your home and into his."

I blinked.

"Oh, that comes as a surprise, child?" she mocked. "I thought you trusted him. Honest and fair. He's been wooing your father for the Cŵn Annwn. One more way to tie you to them."

Behind me, Gabriel cleared his throat. "She's right, Olivia. Well, the part about offering Todd another place to stay. You know Ricky has been out of sorts in his new house. This morning he mentioned he might see whether Todd wanted to be, as he put it, 'roomies' for a while. He was going to ask Todd before speaking to you, which I agreed was correct because…" Another clearing of his throat. "It is Todd's decision."

Not yours. That's what he meant. Hurt and outrage soared in me, and I opened my mouth in protest. Then I shut it. Because Gabriel was correct. Telling me first would have only given me the chance to veto the offer, and I had no right to do that.

I turned to the fae. "Ricky—Arawn—isn't wooing my father. He's trying to help him. To protect him."

She stiffened. "That is my job. Veronica assigned it to *me*. Not to a human boy. Certainly not a Cŵn Annwn boy. I had to rescue your father from this traitor. They argued in the hardware store, and Arawn manhandled him out the back door. Your father tried to escape."

"No, Ricky was getting him away from an actual threat. He was following my father to safety, not chasing him." I sighed. "This is all a misunderstanding. Ask Veronica—"

"Speaking of children," the fae said with a sniff.

"You consider Veronica a child?" I paused. "How old are *you?*"

"Very, very old," said a voice behind me. I turned as Patrick mounted the steps. "Couldn't wait, could you?" He turned to the fae. "Hello, Arianell."

She sniffed again, louder this time, her expression dripping contempt. "Bòcan."

"Yes, it's me, your personal favorite." Patrick glanced at us. "Meet Arianell. As for how old she is, let's just say she was old when they settled Cainsville. She's been a guardian since before your parents were born."

"Guardian?" I said. It hit me then. "The gargoyles. That wasn't just a glamour. She really is a—"

"Gwarcheidwad," Arianell snapped, saying "guardian" in Welsh.

I looked at Patrick. "So, when you *swore* I knew the secret of the gargoyles…"

"I swore nothing of the sort. That was Grace. And I'm sure she didn't swear you knew the *whole* truth. When you accepted a condensed version, she skipped the full one."

"So the gargoyles—the gwarcheidwad—are fae?"

"What did you think they were, Mallt-y-Dydd?" Arianell snapped. "Decorative statuary?"

"They're old fae, aren't they?" I said. "Very, very old fae. Older than the ones in Grace's building."

"It's a way to make them feel useful in their final years," Patrick said. "For some, those final years last a very long time."

Arianell let loose a torrent of Welsh I couldn't follow.

Patrick waved her down. "Yes, yes, Arianell, we all appreciate your dedication to the town."

"*My* town," she said.

"Your town, as one of the founders. You will always have a place here." His eye roll said he wished it to be otherwise. He looked at me. "Wake Ricky up, and get him out of here. Veronica will handle"—he looked at Arianell—"this."

TWENTY-FOUR

OLIVIA

RICKY WAS fine. Pissed off, but fine. I didn't tell him that I knew about the housing offer. I didn't trust myself to be reasonable about it just yet. I settled him onto the sofa with Gabriel, who'd explain the situation with the Kirkmans. Then I went onto the back porch, where Todd crouched beside the deck, examining it.

"The construction of that is driving you nuts, isn't it?" I said.

He smiled and rose.

I handed him a beer. "Miller Genuine Draft."

"Where'd you get it?" he said as he took it. "I read online that it's hard to find."

"I have my ways." I sat on the top step. "So, you're moving in with Ricky."

He winced. He uncapped the beer and took a hit of it. Then he set it down.

"They wouldn't let me see you in prison," he said. "After I was arrested."

I glanced up at him, his expression unreadable as the falling sun backlit his face.

"That day I was arrested," he said, "was the last time I saw you. With your mother also in prison…" He shrugged. "No one would bring you to us. I didn't want you seeing me there, but I wanted…" He shoved his hands in his pockets. "I wanted something. Some closure. All I could think about was the last time you saw us. Dragged away, with no chance to explain it to you. No chance to say we hadn't left you—that we'd never leave you. I was so afraid you'd get angry and forget us." He moved his foot onto the bottom step beside mine. "Which you did."

"I wasn't angry. I was young. I—"

"You were angry and hurt and confused. I'm sure the fae worked magic to help you forget, but part of you wanted to, and I don't blame you. We abandoned you. That's all you knew." He went quiet for a moment and then said, his voice softer, "I will never abandon you again, sweetheart."

I nodded. "If you want to move in with Ricky…"

"I think I should. You and Gabriel might have been together for a year, but it's still a new relationship. I'm in the way." He continued over my protests. "While Gabriel would never even suggest it, we both know this isn't his ideal living situation. The only person he's truly comfortable with is you, and he needs a place where he can close the door and let his guard down."

"We—"

"I'm not offering out of pure altruism, Liv. I need to get back on my feet. I can do that better where I don't have my very competent daughter fretting over my safety. I can take care of myself. You saw that today, I hope." He lowered himself beside me and put an arm around my shoulders. "If you need me to stay a little longer, I will."

Yes, I did need that. I needed to be sure he was okay. But this wasn't about what I needed. In bringing him here, I'd reversed positions